BUYING HIM

THE ROYALS OF AVALONE - INHERITANCE: VICTORIA
PART 1

E.V. DARCY

Copyright © 2021 E. V. Darcy

Cover Design © 2020 Victoria Smith

All rights reserved.

This is a work of fiction. Names, characters, businesses, places, events, and incidents are either the products of the author's imagination or used in a fictitious manner. Any resemblance to actual persons, living or dead, or actual events is purely coincidental.

All rights reserved. No part of this publication may be reproduced, distributed, or transmitted in any form or by any means, including photocopying, recording, or other electronic or mechanical methods, without the prior written permission of the publisher, except in the case of brief quotations embodied in critical reviews and certain other non-commercial uses permitted by copyright law. For permission requests, write to the publisher, addressed "Attention: Permissions Coordinator," at the address below.

Info@evdarcy.com

For all the Ladies looking for their Prince Charming

INTRODUCTION

Before immersing yourself into the world of *The Royals of Avalone*, please allow me to give you some information that will help your experience a little.

The island nation of Avalone resides within the middle of the Atlantic Ocean and is tied loosely to Europe after it broke from English rule in the 1500s. However, it prefers to be self-sufficient, only forming trade deals where it absolutely must, and forgoing any involvement in other nation's military matters. While they are a very insular nation, they hold a particular dislike for their British cousins.

Due to their desire not to be reliant on other nations, Avalone uses the Gold Standard for their economy. Therefore, their money is valued differently to those who use the Dollar Standard.

In Avalone they use *bits, slivers*, and *crowns*, with 100 bits making 1 sliver, and 100 slivers making 1 crown.

A crown is worth 1 gram of gold, so the wealthy citizens of Avalone will often refer to having gold over having money. This is important to note, as at the time of writing the series 1 gram of gold is currently worth approx. £45.00 GB or $60.00 US. This means that having a million crowns is not the same as having a million pounds or dollars! This is something to keep in mind when reading… This is a very wealthy nation, and these are very, *very* wealthy people!

For more information and history of Avalone, please visit www.evdarcy.com.

Enjoy!

King Richard VIII

Grand Duke Harold
- Prince Alistair of Avalone

Princess Helena
- Prince Spencer
- Prince Adam
- Princess Caroline

Duke Alfred
- Prince Leopold
- Prince John

Duke Frederick
- Prince Arthur
- Princess Rebecca
- Princess Francessca

Duke Augustus
- Prince George † Princess Grace
  The first surviving Royal Twins

Princess Amelia
- Princess Jane
- Princess Elizabeth
- Princess Louise
- Prince Hugh

Princess Melinda
- Lady Philippa
- Lady Alexandra
- Lady Victoria
- Lady Henrietta

CHAPTER ONE

'I'm sorry, can you repeat that, please?' Lady Victoria Snape asked, trying to process what the old coot in front of her had just said. The solicitor, the supposed best in all of Avalone, peered over her late father's will at her and her equally flabbergasted sisters, as if his words had been perfectly understandable.

But they couldn't have heard him correctly; their father would *never-*

The lawyer cleared his throat before he repeated, slowly, 'The remaining two-thirds of your father's estate will only be handed down to you and your sisters when—and *if—*you marry before the age of thirty-five.'

Yes, she had heard him right, and yes, her father had indeed screwed them over. What in God's name? Why would he put in such a barbaric clause? They weren't living in Victorian Britain! As had always been the case in Avalone— since they had split from English rule in the sixteenth century—women were treated as equals to men; for as long as men had the right to work and receive an education, women had it too. So why the hell had their father done this?

'Should you do so,' the solicitor continued. 'You will then be granted access to your share of the money-'

'*Access*? What does that mean *access*?' Lady Henrietta enquired, her eyes narrowed.

Victoria, glad her younger sister had picked up on that point, was quickly brought back to there and then, to the finer details of the disgusting clauses their late father had tied to their inheritance.

The lawyer sighed heavily, as if he were dealing with stupid little girls rather than fully grown, well-educated— well perhaps not Victoria—women, and it was starting to get on Victoria's nerves.

'Your Highnesses—'

'*Ladies*,' Lady Philippa corrected the man. 'We are not Royal Highnesses. Never have been, never will be.'

'Speak for yourself,' Lady Alexandra sniffed impetuously. Victoria glared out of the corner of her eye towards her youngest sister. Being rich wasn't the be-all and end-all of their lives, and they were very, *very*, blessed in that department—or had been until their father died—but their youngest sibling wasn't on the same page as her three elder sisters. Alexandra wasn't merely happy with holding the title of Lady, *or* being the daughter of the richest man in Avalone; no, she wanted a crown, and everything their mother hadn't been able to give them.

'Ladies,' Victoria said with a sigh, calling her sisters back to the matter at hand. She rubbed her temples to try to stave off a headache. 'Please, go on, Mr Daven.' She managed a smile of contempt to the self-important twerp who, she was sure, fully supported her father's conditions. Perhaps the bastard had even encouraged them. Maybe *he'd* put the idea in their father's head.

The lawyer nodded, removed his glasses, and began to fiddle with them as he recollected his thoughts. 'Once you marry, the balance of your inheritance—allowing for any interest gains—will be held in a trust under your name. You'll have a yearly stipend from it to ensure that your new family is taken care of-'

'I can look after myself,' Philippa muttered, but quickly bit her tongue when Victoria turned the glare her way. They had no idea how much influence the man had over the trust, but Victoria was certain he had *some* say in it.

'Yes,' Mr Daven nodded. 'Of course you can.' It was clear he didn't really think she could. 'But the stipend will be there should you need it. After the birth of your first child, then you'll—'

'*What*!' Henrietta shrieked, practically jumping from her chair at the final nail in the coffin. 'We're being made to *breed*? Like bloody horse stock? I won't have it,' she shouted, smacking her hand on the solicitor's large wooden desk. 'I am thirty years old. I have attended two of the highest universities the world has to offer. I have a bloody PhD! I have no plans to have children, *ever*. And I will *not* be turned into some man's chattel to get a bit of money and property.'

'Hear, hear!' Philippa stood and joined her sister's side. 'And if you must know, *I* run *2+2*, one of the largest accountancy firms in the country… Actually, don't we do *your* books?'

'If they don't marry, do I get the lot?' Alexandra asked, peering around her older siblings who made noises of disbelief at her question. Victoria merely rolled her eyes, knowing full well of what Alexandra was capable.

The man shifted in his chair, his shoulders straightening, an almost cat's-got-the-cream gleam in his eye as his dry, shrivelled lips twitched in the corner.

'Girls.' Victoria said the single word her sisters knew meant business. Her voice was low, measured, as she eyed the unmoved lawyer; she had a sinking feeling the baby clause wasn't going to be the worst thing they'd hear that day.

'Mr Daven,' Victoria said, feigning politeness. 'Let me get

this completely straight, so that none of us have the slightest misunderstanding. Father left a third of his fortune to charities'—the solicitor's eye twitched at that—'and left each of us an equal share of the remaining half a billion crowns, but we're cut off from it and all its assets—the houses, cars, etcetera—until we marry. And we must marry *before* we turn thirty-five or we'll never see a bit of it. Am I right so far?'

'Quite.'

'And should we marry before the deadline, we'll have *some* access to our inheritance, but we'll only receive *control* of our own fortunes once we bear a child?' Again, the man nodded. Victoria sighed as she rubbed her tired eyes. The unexpected death of their father, the organisation of his funeral, and now... *this,* was starting to take its toll on her. 'So, as Alexi said, what happens to the money should we *not* marry, or produce a child? Is there a time limit on the'—Victoria took a deep breath—'the baby clause?'

Mr Daven met the eyes of each one of them before answering, clearly expecting the fall-out that was about to take place. Victoria wanted to wrap her hands around his scrawny little neck for taking such glee from their predicament.

'Should you marry, you'll have five years to *naturally* produce a child—no adoptions, no fostering, no... *medical* treatments. Should any sister fail to meet any of the stipulations set in the will, their part of the inheritance will be given to the King for—'

All four sisters exploded in a tirade of shock and horror, each declaring their outrage and disbelief that their father would do such a thing. There was no way, Victoria's mind screamed, that their father would give *his* money to his wife's family. A family that had all but disowned her for marrying him in the first place.

'Over my dead body!' Victoria declared, launching herself out of her chair. Mr Daven was unmoved. In fact, it seemed to give him more pleasure, as if he *wanted* her to react in such a manner. 'Those cretins will *never* get my father's money. They treated Mother and Father like dirt and turned us all into outcasts, unworthy of their time or attention. Hell will freeze over before my grandfather, my aunts and uncles, *or* my cousins get their grubby hands on a single sliver of our father's empire.'

'Then you'll have to get married.' Mr Daven said the statement so matter-of-factly Victoria knew there was nothing else they could do. 'And *you*, Lady Victoria, have barely six months. May I ask, are you currently engaged?'

She narrowed her eyes and lifted her chin at the audacity of the man. 'No, I am not.' Even four years after her ex-fiancé had dumped her, it still stung, and she was sure that love was not in her future. It wasn't that she hadn't tried to find someone since. It was just that in comparison to her sisters, her cousins, and even her friends, Victoria wasn't exactly noteworthy for her looks. Or her brains. Not even her career ambitions.

No, there were only two things that endeared Lady Victoria Georgina Snape to men's hearts: her royal connections and her father's money. Maybe it was time to use those assets to her advantage.

She stared at the lawyer who seemed to smirk at her as he slid his spectacles back onto his bony nose.

'I'll have my secretary send you all copies of the stipulations and conditions,' Mr Daven said, peering up at them over the thin, golden frames. 'And the *rules* for each that must be followed.'

'Girls.' Victoria addressed her sisters, but she kept her eyes firmly on the man in front of her. She *would* get married, she vowed as she stood and glared at the solicitor, even if she had to *pay* someone to take her. 'We've got a wedding to plan.'

∾

VICTORIA LOST HERSELF AS SHE WATCHED THE MILK MIX INTO her tea, slowly turning the almost black liquid into a rich, caramel colour. The rattle of a teaspoon against a saucer made her blink as the quiet of the room was disturbed, but her gaze remained on the tiny swirl in the centre of her fine china cup.

She'd always loved watching the spinning twists of the tiny whirlpools, something Mummy had pointed out to her many years ago when she was a child learning the proper etiquette of afternoon tea. Her mother had told her that any problem could be solved with a good cup of tea, that all your troubles and worries disappeared into the vortex when you took your first sip.

Oh, how Victoria wished that were the truth. How everything they'd had dropped on their shoulders that morning could disappear with her first sip of the flavoursome brew, but many years ago she'd learnt Mummy's words were sadly not the truth. She sighed as she lifted the cup from its saucer to take a much-needed sip.

'Relax, Victoria,' Pippa said before taking a drink of her own preferred blend. The heat from the cup steamed her sister's thick glasses, but Pippa paid it no heed. Victoria assumed she was probably used to it after all these years but frowned as she wondered if the glasses were thicker than a few months ago when she'd seen her last. An occupational hazard, Pippa had once told her, a downside to looking at numbers on computer screens all day.

'You'll find someone,' Pippa continued after savouring that first taste of her brew. 'Between the four of us, we've hundreds of eligible men at our disposal. In fact, just the other day, Zach was extolling your virtues after he bumped into you in that little coffee house.'

'Pippa, I'm quite sure he's interested in someone else.'

Victoria threw her sister a wink, knowing how in love Zach, Pippa's assistant, was with his boss. How her sister hadn't realised it, Victoria had no idea.

Pippa frowned. 'No, he definitely said how beautiful you looked. Was going on about the dress you were wearing.' Victoria returned the frown; when she'd bumped into Zach, she'd been wearing her jeans and boots, which she was about to say when Hattie joined the conversation.

'What the hell was Daddy thinking when he wrote that monstrosity of a will?' Victoria and Pippa shook their heads, both just as baffled by their father's actions. 'And to offer it to Grandfather should we not meet the stipulations!' Now it was her turn to frown. 'Do you think he merely did that to ensure we'd go through with the barbaric thing? Because I don't need a man in my life and I certainly don't want kids, but I equally don't want Ol' Dick to get any of Daddy's money.'

'Don't know, don't care. It is what it is,' Alexi said, finally putting her phone down and reaching for her own cup. 'But what I *don't* get is that you're almost thirty-five, Victoria, what if he'd died *after* your birthday? Would he have cut you off?'

Victoria opened her mouth to tell her sister not to be stupid, but promptly closed it again as she considered Alexi's words. Would their father have done that? She wanted to say no, that his unexpected death had merely stopped him from updating his will, from removing something he'd put in years ago, but perhaps he wouldn't have…

Her scowl deepened. It was just so *unlike* her father to put in such a clause in the first place, yet he had; he may well have called her into his office on her birthday and told her she was out of the will.

'Don't be stupid, Alexi,' Hattie snapped, shaking her head at their baby sister. 'Daddy would have ensured that Victoria was taken care of.'

Victoria looked at her sister, aghast at the comment. 'And what the hell does that mean?' she asked. *'Taken care of?'*

It was Pippa who sighed as she put her cup down and looked at Victoria, her face all business. 'Come on, Victoria, don't act like you don't know what Hattie's talking about. You don't have a job—'

'I'm a working royal!'

'—you don't have any qualifications—'

'I have my SEC!' Victoria protested, but even as she said the words, she knew it was a weak argument. The Secondary Education Certificate wasn't difficult to get from *any* Avalonian academy, never mind the awfully expensive private one she'd gone to. Her father had been disappointed she'd not managed to get the Diploma, but at least she'd come away with *something.* School had never been her strong point but put her in a room full of *toffs and what-nots* as Hattie called them, and she knew how to work it.

No, there was no *way* her father would have cut her off. *She'd* been his way into half the deals he'd made over the last decade and a half.

From the age of sixteen, when their mother had sadly passed, Victoria had been *the Lady* of the family. At eighteen, it had fallen upon her slender shoulders to attend all the functions she'd been *required* to as part of their connection to the Avalonian Royal Family—no matter how unwanted she might be. The parties, galas, boring state dinners, the over-the-top weddings and long-drawn-out funerals, and everything and anything else *they* deemed she was required to attend to represent their mother's legacy.

Victoria had made sure she had never caused a fuss, never raised her head above the parapet, had ensured she never gave her grandfather any reason to dislike her, but it never mattered. It seemed just being her father's daughter, a reminder she wasn't the product of a match the King had deemed worthy, was enough to earn his derision and scorn.

He'd sneer at her every time she was presented, his nose wrinkling like a bad smell had suddenly invaded his hairy nostrils.

So, while Victoria had not been the brightest of the Snape sisters, the forced attendance at the royal events gave her access to connections her father had *needed*. She'd heard things, seen things; she knew who was doing what, where they were doing it, and when it was happening, all because no one thought that dim little she could possibly be a problem. She was merely an ornament, another socialite who lived off her daddy's money, and added a sparkle of beauty to the room.

Well, perhaps not the last part. The papers, glossy magazines, and news shows, not even her father had ever described *her* as a beauty. Marcus had always said she was pretty, cute, adorable even, but never beautiful. But that wasn't the point.

The point was, *she'd* been her daddy's ear. Plain old Victoria had been her father's tip-off on deals being made and who was backstabbing whom. However, such work wasn't suitable for a resume; attending parties to gain information didn't give her any employable skills.

The cold, hard reality was Victoria was completely screwed if she didn't get her inheritance.

'And *there* it is,' Hattie said, lifting her teacup as if toasting the revelation. 'The bit's finally dropped.'

'*Merde*,' Victoria breathed, not even bothering to look abashed about the use of such a word. 'Do you think he's done it to make us stand on our own feet?'

'Really?' Pippa said, gazing at Victoria over the top of her teacup. She slid her eyes towards Hattie before looking back at Victoria. 'Perhaps, for you and Alexi.'

'Hey!' Alexi protested. 'I keep telling you guys, I'll be a queen one day.' Victoria, Pippa, and Alexi rolled their eyes and groaned in unison at the words they'd grown tired of hearing. 'You can mock me all you want,' Alexi said haughtily. 'But you mark my words, I *will* be a queen.'

'Yes, *Your Majesty*,' Victoria said. 'Just don't try and bonk Alistair, okay?'

'Ew! We're cousins!'

'At least she has *some* boundaries,' Pippa sniffed. Her comment made Hattie snort into her cup. Victoria bit back a smile as she watched her sister's cheeks flush bright red at her lack of decorum; she wasn't a total heathen after all.

'But, before you go and rule whatever great nation you've set your sights upon,' Pippa continued. 'We need to put ourselves on the back-burner and ensure that Victoria's share doesn't go to King Richard.'

'Hear, hear!' Hattie said.

'I'd rather be beheaded for treason than see *him* getting my money,' Victoria said defiantly as she picked up her cup before taking a sip of her drink. 'But I'm afraid that it may end up being the case.'

'What?' Hattie asked, her head turning sharply to her elder sibling. 'Why? As Pippa just said, we'll help. Between us, we know a plethora of men; we'll find you someone.'

'Oh, what about those friends of yours—Jensen or Roman Tyrrell?' Alexi piped up. 'They're handsome *and* independently wealthy. They'll need their own heirs and old man Tyrrell would *kill* to get his hands on some of Daddy's assets.'

They certainly were handsome, but Jensen Tyrrell was a womanising wild man, who Victoria didn't think could be counted on and had caused many problems between Hattie and their father. And the few times Victoria had met his twin Roman, he'd been cold and aloof to everyone present. There was no warmth to him; what would he be like as a husband and father? She was about to shake her head *no* when Hattie beat her to it.

'No.' Her voice was firm and brooked no room for argument. Colour rose to tinge her cheeks pink as all three pairs of eyes turned to focus on her, brows raised in surprise at the amount of venom held in a single word. 'I mean, Jensen's sworn he'll never marry and Roman has a long-term girlfriend, Fiona Martin.'

'Ugh, I *hate* the Martins,' Alexi said, stirring her tea with a silver spoon. 'I heard she's as cold as a fish. Maybe he'd be willing to give her up in exchange for something.' Hattie narrowed her eyes at her youngest sister.

'You're all forgetting one thing,' Victoria said with a sigh, before Hattie could answer. 'We're in *mourning*, I can't find a husband if we're locked away for six months as we were when mother died.'

The rattle of Hattie's cup hitting the table, the splash of tea over the edges pooling in the saucer made the other three Snape Ladies turn their attentions back to their sister. Hattie glared at Victoria as she pulled her legs from under her and sat forward. '*You* were locked away,' she spat, and Victoria recoiled from the heat within her words. '*I* was shipped off to school in Guildford—remember? That's how I know Roman, Jensen, Fiona and any of the others you want to try and jump into bed with.'

'Hattie, we don't mean it like that.' Pippa tried to soothe their younger sibling as Victoria swallowed at the memory of watching the maids filling suitcases with Hattie's clothes, and Hattie, still distraught from Mummy's death, begging Daddy —literally on her knees in front of him—not to send her away. Victoria had argued with him for months afterwards, pleading with him to bring her home, but it had all fallen on deaf ears.

'I'm sorry,' Victoria whispered.

Hattie sniffed, throwing her curly hair over her shoulder and turning her face away slightly, but Victoria swore she caught the shimmer of unshed tears in her eyes.

'You're head of the house now, Tori'—Victoria glared at Pippa's use of an endearment she hadn't heard in years

—'Victoria, sorry. But I am right; you're head of the house, you set the mourning period for us. If you only want a month—'

'Two weeks,' Hattie said, refusing to meet anyone's gaze as she stood up. 'I say two weeks and we just get on with it. I've never understood such a stupid tradition anyway,' she informed them as she moved towards the door. Pippa's butler, Giles, appeared without prompting, with her coat ready. 'He's gone, we're not, let's keep going.'

'Hattie, please—'

'*Two weeks*, Victoria,' Hattie said as she fastened her coat, still not meeting her sisters' eyes. 'I'll see you in fifteen days at Dick's birthday celebration.' And with that, she turned and left the room, leaving the remaining three sisters to stare after her.

'Wow,' Alexi said as she put her own cup back on the table between them. 'She's still pissed at Daddy for sending her away.'

'Wouldn't you have been?' Victoria asked, staring after her departed sister. As Pippa shifted in her seat and Alexi coughed politely, Victoria knew she was asking the wrong sisters; Pippa had done everything she could to keep up with Hattie's intellect, desperate to get on the same programme as the thirteen-year-old and failing, while Alexi had felt like a prisoner within the walls of Renfrew Hall at just six years old, all her friends forbidden to come and play with her.

'Fine.' Victoria's cup rattled as she put it carelessly on the table and shoved it away from her before she, too, stood up to leave. 'Two weeks from now. I'll see you all at the birthday celebrations.'

'Victoria wait—'

'Oh, come on—'

Pippa and Alexi's cries fell on deaf ears as she left without even waiting for her coat.

The roar of the crowds from beyond the gates below was thunderous as the large glass doors, leading to the balcony of the Grand Palace, slid open. Victoria and her three sisters stepped out onto the stone terrace, the lowest-ranking members of the Royal Family always the first to face the cheering crowds on public holidays. Victoria wanted to shrink back, to recoil and hide from the horde below. She spied the telescopic cameras atop the news platforms in the middle of the filled boulevard that led to the palace gates.

She didn't see any flashes from them—pointless at such a distance—but she knew they were eagerly snapping away at the foursome as they confidently strode into public again after just two weeks of mourning, the shortest in the Royal Family's history. She knew the event was being broadcast live, that homes across the nation—and the world—would be watching their appearance on their television screens with newscasters voicing aloud the question they were all thinking; surely it was too soon for the four Snape Ladies to be here. Even the most die-hard of royalists out there, knowing how important the King's ninetieth birthday celebration was to the nation as the world's longest-reigning monarch, would find their short-lived mourning period distasteful. But while Victoria would love to settle into a long, traditional time away from the world's prying eyes, come tomorrow she had to get ready to start seeking a husband.

Of course, the world would never know it was actually Daddy's fault they'd had to break with tradition. They'd never know he was forcing his daughters to marry and breed, and that by his stupid time frame he was forcing his eldest to marry someone who'd amount to nothing more than a stranger.

She internally cringed at the thought of what the press were going to say over the next few months. Her father dies and only a fortnight later she's off courting any Tom, Dick, or Harry. She fought off wrinkling her nose; she'd have to get her secretary to cross off anyone on the list with such names. Best to avoid giving the press any easy headlines.

The cheering started again, rowdier and louder than it had been before as the four of them reached the solid stone railing and into full view.

Victoria waved at those below, her sisters on either side, before they split into pairs; she and Alexi moving to the right, and Pippa and Hattie to the left to make way for Jane, Louise, Elizabeth, and Hugh, the next rung up on the royal ladder.

Each set of her younger cousins would appear, immediately followed by their parents, with Prince Alistair of Avalone and the Grand Duke and Duchess making their appearance just before the King.

Although today's holiday was an extra special event, all public holidays were graced with the presence of the Royal Family; the people of Avalone were loyal to the monarchy and proud of their heritage and history. They boasted they were the only country with a true ruling monarchy left in Europe, leaving other kings and queens merely puppets of their respective states, figureheads with no real purpose other than to be national trinkets, rolled out to play nice to those with power when they visited their country; courtiers, in their own home, courtesans for their politicians.

And while royal houses had changed throughout Europe over the centuries—Britain had gone through the House of Tudor to the current house of Buckingham, passing through many European branches on the way—the House of Grey had ruled Avalone since the sixteenth century when Queen Jane had been spirited away from the chopping block under the orders of the future Queen Elizabeth of England.

Victoria had always shared these feelings; proud her nation stood tall and still carried the true blood of kings and queens in their veins. She just wished she weren't so directly part of the establishment, that she could be one of the people who stood outside the gates, enjoying it jubilantly and unaware of the ins and outs of the infighting of the family, ignorant of its flaws and traditions. She wasn't sure her grandfather knew *she* was aware of the unspoken traditions, of the secret they'd hidden away for hundreds of years. But she did know, and once she'd found out, she'd promised she'd keep it hidden from her siblings, protecting them from the audacity of it all. She also knew if her sisters found out the true depths their family would go to, to maintain the status quo of their perfection in the eyes of the public, the secrets would be spilt.

Hell, Hattie would shout them from the balcony, screaming to the crowd below at the top of her lungs, consequences be damned.

Victoria shifted her eyes, casting a glance at her sister across the terrace. Hattie held the prescribed shadow of a smile as she waved at the crowds, but her glassy and vacant gaze showed she was far from the proceedings. Victoria held back the sigh she wanted to heave. Ever since Hattie had been half-dragged away to Guildford University, there had been a distance between the third Snape sister and the rest of them. Nothing Victoria tried had worked, and the rift had only intensified every time Hattie was made to attend a royal function or event. Victoria was sure that if Hattie was given the option, she'd cut herself off from every member of her family—including her sisters—and hide away somewhere with just her computer and an internet connection so she could work.

Victoria was brought back to the moment as the cheering became those hysterical screams of excitement that only a woman could make when their heartthrob entered their view. Without glancing back, Victoria knew her cousin Alistair had stepped into sight. The Prince of Avalone, second in line to the throne, had tickled the fancy of many a woman from his teenage years. His pictures had become pin-up posters in teenage magazines growing up, much to his chagrin, and endless amusement and jealousy from his other cousins. At twenty-eight years old and still unmarried, there were always rumours of who his wife and future queen would be.

Victoria's heart ached for her younger cousin, trapped more than she was by the bindings of royalty and unable to do a thing about it without dire consequences for the nation's stability. He'd often come to her drunk, spilling secrets she knew their grandfather would hang anyone else for revealing and confessing how he hated everything about his lineage and the trappings it came with, that he'd give up the crown and everything it came with for a normal, simple life.

But she had no time to dwell on the misfortune her favourite cousin had in his future; in a few moments, after the Grand Duke appeared, the chants of *God Save The King* would start and she'd have to face her grandfather for the first time in months. He hadn't even had the decency to attend her father's funeral.

Victoria felt the grind of her teeth sliding over one another as the chants began. The hand at her side, hidden from the view of the crowds below by the stone balustrade, curled tightly into a fist. Although His Majesty was always the focus of such events, he never showed himself to the rest of the family before he entered the balcony.

Running the country means there isn't time for standing around and making idle chit-chat, her mother had once explained when Victoria had been but a tiny child at her first public holiday and asked where her grandfather was. *Up until the moment he walks through those doors, he's being told information about the country and being asked what everyone else should do.*

And what should everyone do, Mummy? she'd enquired in her innocence.

Whatever the King says, her mother had said, standing up and smoothing down her dress before they had walked onto the balcony, her tiny hand clenched in her mother's.

She heard the low whistle from one of the footmen announcing the King's arrival, and just like a trained dog, she turned to face the grand doors before dropping into a low curtsy and holding it.

'My bloody knees,' Alexi said, her voice a quiet whisper to Victoria's ear, but Victoria knew her sister was shouting to be heard over the roar of the crowd. 'I swear when I'm a queen, I will never make anyone do this for such a stupid amount of time. A short dip will be plenty long enough.'

Victoria gently knocked her sister's elbow, silently warning her to keep her thoughts to herself, especially at such a public event.

'Oi!' Alexi sounded indignant but returned the nudge with one of her own. If Victoria hadn't been practising her pose every night before bed for the last fortnight, knowing she was well out of practice, she would have fallen over.

The King's arrival at the balustrade was the cue for the family to rise from their prolonged bows and curtsies and return to the attention of the masses far below, and Victoria was able to turn to her sister and drop her words directly into her ear. 'Queens never complain in public. It isn't dignified.'

She didn't wait for a response, turning back to the crowds and the news outlets with their prying cameras and recording equipment, but from the corner of her eye she saw Alexi's chin rise ever so slightly. The serene ghost of a smile Victoria had taught her siblings years ago brushed her perfectly painted lips. Victoria didn't for one moment believe Alexi would ever actually become a queen, but if she did have the good fortune to have her wish granted, Victoria believed she'd make the picture-perfect consort beside her husband.

'We shouldn't even be here,' she heard Alexi say anyway, and knew her sister was trying to get a rise out of her. She always did once she was put in her place.

But in this instance, her sister was right; they should be in their homes mourning their father's death, no matter how much Hattie and he had butted heads. Or that he thought his eldest needed a man to come along and take care of her. Or that he forbade Alexi to follow the royal circuit despite her desires. Or that he always showed his disappointment in Pippa for wanting to start her own business rather than entering his… Victoria mentally sighed. No matter all that, they should still be there, mourning their father. But right now, this was their lot in life, and unless she found a husband, this would be it for the rest of hers.

CHAPTER TWO

The world started to tilt as Victoria all but stumbled across the car park, trying to get away from Simon. The man had been a buffoon all evening, a horrible chauvinistic *pig,* who thought he was God's gift to the planet, and for that reason alone, was owed everything he wanted in life. She was going to *kill* Alexi when she got home.

If she got home.

That thought scared the living daylights out of her and spurred her shaking legs on. But, as she heard her pursuer huffing and puffing as he tried to move his heavy frame as fast as he could to catch up to her, she realised such a horrible sentiment might become reality.

Fine, she'd haunt her sister's arse and whatever palace the damn wannabe-queen ended up in. She hoped it was small and cold, with an army of ghosts she could sway to terrorise her youngest sibling.

'Victoria! Wait!' Simon called out. She sent a prayer of thanks to the Heavens that even as messed up as her head was, she was able to outrun him. Although, she wasn't sure for how much longer.

What in God's name had he done to her? *Why* was her

head so screwy? It had to be something he'd done as she'd purposefully only had one glass of wine and that had been *with* her meal, so she couldn't be drunk. She certainly didn't feel-

Her vision went blurry, and she staggered to the left as the world decided to tip to one side without warning... Although, that might be because her head suddenly felt too heavy for her neck and it decided it wanted to meet the floor. Luckily, a car broke her fall.

Her hands slammed onto the bonnet of the vehicle first, stopping her body from smashing into it, but not from collapsing on top of the cold, hard metal, and setting off the car's alarm.

The blearing, screaming siren startled her mind, clearing the fog just enough so she could turn herself over and get back to her feet. But it was a short-lived effect; the world started to dim again as she spied her pursuer's super-sized frame stop under a streetlight not far from her.

Simon's gaze fell on her, his eyes narrowing and his thin lips seeming to disappear altogether as he scowled at her. He didn't seem perturbed by the screeching alarm, too focused on his prey trying to slip through his fingers.

'Why'd you have to run?' he asked, leaning against the lamppost to try and catch his breath. Victoria hoped he had a heart attack. 'If you'd just got in the damned car, you'd have passed out in comfort...'

He *had* given her something.

Victoria tried to speak, wanted to tell him exactly what she thought of him as the darkness crept into the corners of her vision. But her tongue was too heavy, her mouth tasted like it was filled with cotton wool and she was trying to stay standing.

Her brain tried to comfort her, telling her it was a valiant effort as the strength disappeared from her knees. Simon became almost two feet taller than just moments before, and her mind thought how strange it was to know that her knees had connected to the road, yet she hadn't felt a thing.

She'd done a good job trying to get away from the creep, but it wasn't enough. She shouldn't have allowed herself to get into this position in the first place. If Marcus could see her now, he'd stand there tutting at her, shaking his head and listing all the things she'd failed to do that night to keep herself safe. But she'd take her ex-fiancé being an utter bastard to her while saving her arse over giving Simon everything he'd been alluding to wanting all evening.

Her.

The darkness no longer crept into her vision but slithered through it as her kneeling body swayed. The devil gathered himself together and stepped towards her. She wanted to punch the smug grin right off his face.

Her last thought before she passed out was that she hoped her sisters would mourn her for more than two weeks…

CHAPTER THREE

'Cormac!' Geri shouted down the corridor just as he fell onto the break room sofa for his fifteen minutes of respite. 'Your car's alarm is going bloody nuts-o again.'

Cormac groaned, wondering what the hell else could go wrong this evening. He'd been late to work and thus banned from the main stage, and to top it all off, it appeared he'd been ripped off on the repairs on his piece of shit car.

'On it!' he shouted back, pulling himself up from the crappy couch. Grabbing the keys to his little Volkswagen from his already open locker, he stumbled out of the break room and into the narrow corridor, cursing the new layout of the club again.

The money is made out there, he remembered Britney saying when the staff had complained the remodelling had made the employees' area smaller than before. *More space, more customers, more tips for you*, the boss had countered.

Cormac ran down the short set of stairs at the back of the club, the clanging of his feet on the metal steps echoing down the empty stairwell. He frowned as his ears picked up the screeching alarm. He was going to just rip the damn thing out of the rusty, too small Beetle and be done with it. The piece of crap wasn't ever likely to get stolen anyway, and if it did, well, the thieves would be doing him a favour!

He pushed open the staff door at the back of the building and stepped out into the employee car park. He swore if some kids were—

'What the fuck?' he said without thinking as he took in the scene of a man leaning over what looked like a woman spread halfway under his car… Hell, had his car rolled forward and hit someone? He was going to sue the arse off the garage if that was the case. He'd *told* them the handbrake needed fixing.

The guy jerked upright at Cormac's voice, twisting around in surprise at the disturbance. The stranger's beady eyes grew wide at Cormac's large frame, probably made all the more foreboding by the light spilling from the building's entrance behind him. He probably looked like a hulking shadowy beast, and even in the pallid yellow light of the nearby lampposts, Cormac saw the man's face drain of colour.

Definitely *not* a Good Samaritan situation.

'She alright, buddy? You need a hand?' he called as he stepped towards the couple without waiting for an invitation. The man's tiny eyes darted down to the woman and back to him, and Cormac knew the guy was about to turn and run—

Okay, in reality it was more like a waddle, and while Cormac knew he could easily chase the bastard down—a three-legged, half-dead turtle probably could—he was aware he needed to check on the woman first.

It took four attempts to switch the stupid alarm off as he jogged over to his car, with the noise finally ceasing a moment before he reached the damsel in distress. He crouched down, brushing back the woman's long dark hair that had fallen over her face, and held his hand in front of her mouth to ensure she was still breathing. Thankfully, she was.

He gently turned the woman over and managed to get his arms behind her neck and knees, easily lifting her as he stood. He wasn't dealing with this shit out here; poor woman had enough problems, being a public spectacle didn't have to be one of them. As he headed back to the building, he noted that although she wasn't short, the mystery lady barely weighed anything; a diminutive thing like her wouldn't have stood a chance against the hefty prick who'd been towering over her.

As Cormac climbed the stairs towards the staff lounge, he shuddered at the thought of what might have happened to her if he hadn't arrived when he did. It was bloody lucky his alarm was messed up or he wouldn't have known about the whole thing until the club had shut and the staff headed home. Hell, that was *hours* from now and who knew what could have happened in that time; would she have even still been there? The guy could very well have taken her if Cormac hadn't interrupted.

'Geri!' he shouted down the corridor as he reached the break room. 'Get here, now! And bring the first aid kit!'

He kicked the door to the staff room open and stepped inside, thankful he'd been put on a solo break. He didn't want the woman to be the talk of the town before *she* even knew what'd happened.

He placed her on the old, tatty couch, gently resting her head on the only pillow it offered. He brushed her hair back behind her ear, his hand caressing her jawline before falling away. Despite the graze along her left cheekbone, her skin was beautiful; clear and radiant, and so soft. He reached up to trail his fingers along her cheek again…

'What's the prob— Who's she?' Geri said, making him jump guiltily as she came strolling into the lounge.

'Dunno,' he said with a shrug as he checked the mysterious woman over for any signs that she'd been assaulted in any way. Her dress—which even *he* recognised as expensive—was still fastened, her shoes were on properly, so no struggle, and her tights, although there were bits of dirt on her knees, didn't *look* like they'd been disturbed… and the thought that perhaps they had been, made his stomach drop.

Hell, if he ever got his hands on that bastard, he'd wring his puffed-up neck!

'Hey, Geri, do me a solid, just check under her dress to make sure it's all… still there.'

He felt the bookkeeper go still behind him. Yeah, it wasn't a standard request, and he was sure that to anyone else it would sound perverted, but he had to know if he had got there in time. Had he managed to spare her at least that heartbreak? He was going on a manhunt as soon as he possibly could—and he was sure the rest of the boys at the club would happily join him—but he needed to know if they had to kill the prick or just break every bone in his fat body.

'What?' she squeaked. 'What the hell happened?'

'I'm not entirely sure, but I *think* she's been drugged. The graze looks more like it came from the floor than a fist, and I can't smell alcohol on her breath, so I don't think she's been drinking…'

'Hells bells,' Geri breathed as she stepped forward. 'And you think she might have been messed with?'

'Guy was standing over her in front of my car,' Cormac said, eyes still on the unconscious woman. He refused to move from her side, even as Geri stood beside him to take a quick peek. The blue-haired woman swallowed before she carefully lifted the woman's skirt up with two fingers, just enough to check if anything untoward had happened, before she quickly dropped it again.

'All intact there; tights still up properly!' she said as she quickly stepped away again, running her hands through her short hair. 'Obvs I'm not an expert, but I'd say you got there before the perv could do anything like… *that*. I'll go call the fuzz.'

Cormac released the breath he'd been holding, and rolled his neck across his shoulders, wincing at the crunching noise that ground through his bones.

He returned his attention to the unconscious beauty. She was tall with a slim frame; her tiny shoulders were bare, and her skin was a beautiful peach colour. She had long, dark lashes, and a plump, lush mouth that just begged to be tasted. For a moment, the thought of kissing her drifted through his mind, waking her like the princesses in the films he watched with his little brother, James…

He took a step back and turned around, his hands grabbing the back of his neck as he tried to regain his composure. He pulled at the collar around his neck, the Velcro giving way easily, and threw it to the other side of the room. He'd just rescued her from a potential sexual assault, and there he was daydreaming of doing the same exact thing as Pervy McPervface!

Hell, he'd always thought the princes in those fairy tale films were creepy as hell; he'd tried to explain such a fact to his six-year old brother, that the princes should *ask* the princesses if they wanted to be kissed, but James just looked at him as if he was hopeless.

It's a fairy tale, had been his childlike, matter-of-fact answer, *not real life, Corrie. And* how *can the prince ask if she's* asleep? The *duh* had been silent.

He wondered if anyone had tried that explanation in court? He could imagine the lawyers trying to call it the *Sleeping Beauty Defence.*

He glanced over his shoulder towards the mystery woman as she groaned and shifted her head in her sleep, and his eyes unwittingly travelled down her body. Her breasts were small but pert and round, her hips flared ever so gently, and he wondered if the peachy colour of her shoulders was true for the rest of her body.

He blinked at the thought and turned his lip up in disgust at himself. Man, he *had* to get out there and meet someone, or at least get laid soon. His next night off, he was going out and meeting someone, for real this time. Ogle some women in a bar, *conscious* women who'd stare back at him, rather than poor, vulnerable, unconscious women.

He popped out of the staff room, to give himself a second to get his head straight and took the chance to shout to Geri to *hurry the fuck up*.

'What the hell is up with you tonight?' she asked as she came bouncing along the corridor again, a jangle of chains and piercings, her hair drifting between purple and blue as the light shifted over it. 'You'd think you resent being a hero.'

'Hero? I'm not a hero,' he said, narrowing his eyes at his co-worker. There were times he really wanted to put his finger through her bullring and yank it. Today was one of those days. 'I just found her.'

'You *do* know who that is, don't you?' Geri asked as she squeezed past him to get a better look at their guest.

'No.' He took his own step towards the sleeping princess, a frown pulling his brows together. He didn't recognise her, but there was a hint of familiarity.

'She an actress or something?' he asked.

'Are you kidding me? Get your head out your arse and start taking in what's going on in the world outside this place. *That's* Lady Victoria Snape,' Geri said in disbelief, pointing at the stranger.

'Bullshit,' he scoffed, but he glanced towards the woman with curiosity. 'Lady Snape's like what, forty? And that woman's not even thirty.'

'Aw, she'll be happy to hear that when she wakes up,' Geri

mocked, rolling her eyes at him. '*Not only did I* not *get sexually assaulted this evening,*' she said in a faux-upper class voice, holding her hand to her throat. '*A man thinks I'm five years younger than I really am! My skin care regime is really working!*' She stood on her tiptoes and whacked him on the back of the head, making him yelp and glare at her.

'Dude, you're probably going to get like a heap of cash from her as a reward. Oh! Maybe King Richard will knight you and give you a big house somewhere!' The impish woman started to bounce on her feet.

'Well, if that happens, I'll ensure to stop by here every day so you have to *bow* to me.'

'You'll kiss my arse before I bow to you,' she said, and Cormac knew she spoke the truth. He highly doubted he'd get anything of the nature—he wasn't that lucky—but a small reward wouldn't be refused by him. A few crowns would certainly help to pay the mountain of bills he'd piled high recently. If he could just clear the rent arrears, he'd be laughing.

He was about to ask Geri if she seriously thought he might get something when his friend's whole body suddenly went rigid. 'Oh, bollocks! You don't think they were trying to *kidnap* her, do you?'

Cormac considered her question for a moment, his mind recalling with perfect clarity the scene he'd stepped into. The man had been standing over Lady Snape, moving down to bended knee. He moved his thoughts passed the guy, trying to remember the surroundings; no cars or vans were running nearby, the barrier to the car park was still lowered…

'Nah,' he said, shaking his head. 'There was only the one bloke.'

Geri wrinkled her nose in disgust, a clear sign she was about to rant about something, but the hammering of feet on the metal stairs stopped her before she began. The two turned to the doorway just as Nick popped his head around the frame.

'Geri!' he panted, looking happy to see the woman until his eyes grazed over the sleeping princess—quite literally, it appeared—between them. 'Holy shit, it's true!'

'What?' the duo asked, almost in unison.

'The Lady Snape, she's here! Axel sent me up to see if they could be right before he called the boss.' Despite not having a clue what his co-worker was talking about, Cormac groaned at the idea of Britney coming all the way down to the club on her night off. If she did, there'd be hell to pay.

'There's a load of police officers downstairs,' Nick continued. '*And* the Royal Guard—the *head* of the Guard is here!'

Cormac groaned. That was all they needed. The elite task force in charge of the security and safety of the Royal Family on the premises was going to put a huge mark on the business and not for the right reasons. Britney was going to go berserk when she found out and have all their hides for it.

'They're threatening to raid the place if they don't get to see the Lady Snape. I'll send them up. Perhaps Brit won't come then.'

'No, wait,' Cormac said, stepping forward. 'We've got to handle this carefully; send only the Head of the Guard up and two *female* officers. No one else, I don't care what they say to you. Get Axel and Davy to stand their ground; they know the legalise of them being on the premises without warrants.' Nick nodded along to all his requests and Cormac wondered if he was giving the bloke too much to do. He was useless at taking the easiest of drink orders from customers on a slow night. If Nick hadn't been the best looking of them all, Cormac was sure he'd have been fired long ago.

'Offer the rest mineral waters and soft drinks in the Green Room—that's available this evening, isn't it, Geri?'

'Um, yeah.' The girl stared up at him as if she had no clue who he was. Cormac internally scowled; he could take charge when he had to—he'd just saved a princess, for crying out loud. Nick nodded and disappeared back down the stairs.

Cormac dragged his hand down his face as he glanced back at the woman—*no, Lady Snape*—on the couch. Her body shivered slightly in the cool room, and without thinking, Cormac grabbed his coat off the peg and stepped towards her. He hesitated as he held it over her and took another look at her pretty face.

A heavy ball of worry sat in his stomach; he'd just got caught up in something and this was something *big*. He'd already thought his life was a mess, but he had the sinking feeling it was about to get a whole lot messier.

∼

VICTORIA SNUGGLED DOWN FURTHER DOWN INTO HER BED AS the wisps of sleep were whisked away from her. She groaned in disapproval as voices, although muffled, pulled her further away from the land of slumber. She wanted one night, one night of peaceful sleep…

Actually, one night of sleep full stop would be a blessing, she mused, thinking of how she hadn't had more than a few hours of restless slumber since her father had passed away. She'd spent most of her nights going over the mess the will had left her in, trying to figure out what she'd do if she wasn't able to fulfil its stipulations. On nights she had dates, she went over them in excruciating detail afterwards, trying to determine if her suitor that night was worth meeting up again. So far, she'd had only three men make it to date number two and none of them had managed to reach any further.

She frowned as the voices grew louder, clearer, and she knew she wasn't going to get any more sleep that night, no matter how much her foggy mind was trying to pull her back into the waiting arms of the Sandman. She'd have to have a word with Berryman in the morning about the staff being noisy.

Pulling the covers tighter around her, she tried to snuggle further into the bed. A spring was sticking into the bottom of her back and she needed to—

She sighed happily as she managed to get the right angle to avoid the spring and better still, the voices became silent. She smiled sleepily into the soft, warm blanket, breathing deeply the wonderful rich scent it carried. She'd have to compliment Helen in the morning on the wonderful fragrance she'd had the sheets dusted with—far better than the usual overly flowery smell the laundry maids always used.

'She's waking up,' an unfamiliar voice said, making Victoria crack her eyes open.

Dammit!

The light was bright and made her head thump. Her stomach wanted to turn inside out at the painful pulsing at her temples, and her mouth tasted as if it already had. She stuck her tongue out in disgust and wrinkled her nose. She needed painkillers and a toothbrush, pronto.

'Hey, you okay?' a deep, male voice asked. It set her on high alert. She knew every member of staff at Renfrew Hall and what they sounded like. It was all part of the security protocols in case anyone tried-

Unknown voices. Uncomfortable bed. Unfamiliar smells...

Oh, God. She'd been *kidnapped!*

'Are you okay?' the voice enquired again. 'Do you want some water?'

She wanted to shake her head *no*, but she knew if she did it would likely explode. And then there were the rules security had drilled into her over the years...

Do whatever they say.

Accept kindnesses, lest they become angry at you.
Look at everything you can.
And if you can't see, listen*!*

She gave her captor a weak thumbs-up out of the side of the blanket to his question, and listened intently to his heavy footfall as he moved around. There wasn't carpet on the floor and the slightly sticky footsteps made her already queasy stomach clench uneasily. She tried to open her mouth to alleviate the cotton wool feeling that filled it and cringed as she felt the skin on her lips slowly pulling apart. Seriously, what the hell had happened? How had they managed to take her? She built up the courage to ask the questions when a cool glass was gently pressed against her dry mouth.

She jumped at the contact and the water sloshed over her lips, wetting her mouth and chin, and dribbling down her neck. But she paid it no heed as soon as the cool, crisp water touched her tongue; her body went on instinct and tried to take as much as it could. It was better than the most expensive champagne, more exquisite than the finest wine she'd ever supped, and she wanted it *all*.

'Sip it, don't guzzle,' the voice said softly, pulling the glass back slightly so she couldn't get to it. She swallowed the water in her mouth and mewed in displeasure, reaching blindly for the glass and sticking her now wet lip out in a pout. She *needed* that water; it was the only thing in the world that would make her head stop pounding, her throat stop feeling like it was made of sandpaper, and her stomach acting like it was on the high seas during the worst storm ever recorded.

'Fuck,' the voice breathed before the glass was shoved back at her mouth. It clipped her teeth, making her wince and groan. Her hand flew up between the glass and her face to rub at her lip and the voice swore again. 'I'm sorry,' it muttered, and Victoria once more tried to peel her eyes open to see her carer.

The light was bright, and her eyes wanted to fight against her, but slowly she forced them open and made them focus on the first thing she saw…

A divine-looking man sat at her side, his hip pressing against hers, a spot of warmth on the otherwise cold leather couch. She met his mossy-green eyes that crinkled in the corners as his lips turned upwards into a tentative smile.

She tried to think if she'd seen him before; Marcus said that kidnappers were likely to have run into their mark at some point as they tried to establish their target's routine. Some would even converse with their prey, try to get to know them to make any attempt easier.

She didn't recall seeing *this* man any time recently. She was certain she'd remember those eyes, the fullness of his mouth, the way his freckles dusted his nose…

Freckles. She stared at them. She almost reached out to try and touch them, to count them as her mind began to drift lazily back towards the fog rather than focusing on the matter at hand.

Slowly, Victoria turned her head, keeping her eyes on him for a moment longer before she finally took in where she was. She raised a well-maintained brow at the state of the place. Whatever the room was supposed to be, it looked more like a junk yard-cum-building site than anything else. Everything, including the couch she'd been deposited on, seemed to be covered in a layer of dirt, grime, or grease.

Oh, God, she was *lying* on it!

She didn't think of the consequences, didn't consider that if she tried to get off the couch they may tie her up, handcuff her to the radiator so she had to sit on the floor—she swore those were mice droppings down by the pipes—or even lock her away in a dark cupboard somewhere, but she had to get off that filthy thing right *now*!

Her captor stood with her and held out a hand to help her up, but without thinking, she batted it away. She paused in her scramble to get up, fearing a smack for her action, but the man merely sighed and nothing more. No ranting, no screaming, no threats to do something to her. He simply put the glass of water he was still holding on the tiny table in front of them before standing nearby, ready to catch her when she started to sway.

Okay, perhaps she *should* have accepted his help. She reached out with one hand, and the man instantly offered his arm to steady her.

Where was she? Why was she here? And what the bloody hell had happened for her to feel like she'd been hit by a car?

Crap, *had* she been hit by a car? Was that how they'd got her here? Why couldn't she remember anything? And why was her captor shirtless, covered in what looked like baby oil, and wearing trousers so tight she wondered if they'd been painted on? The tiny, pointless cuffs at each wrist made her frown deepen. What the hell was going on?

'What… happened?' she finally croaked as she looked up at the stranger—damn, he was tall. Usually, at her height, she didn't need to tilt her head back to look at a guy. However, this one could probably throw her over his shoulder and haul her off somewhere without effort at all. Had he carried her here?

'You don't remember anything?' the stranger asked.

'You've kidnapped me.' She narrowed her eyes at him in challenge. This wasn't the first kidnapping attempt made against her, and sadly she knew it wouldn't be the last, but it was certainly the most successful. No one had ever *actually* got away with her before.

However, that didn't mean she was going to be an easy captive; she'd make them rue the day they took her.

'You won't get anything from King Richard if that's your aim. No money, no bargaining—no negotiations what-so-ever.' The man frowned, his smooth brow furrowing, his nose wrinkling ever so slightly, making those hypnotic freckles dance. 'And my father's money is tied up,' she continued. 'The company is off limits too, embroiled in so much red tape until the will is settled that it would be a nightmare to try and get anything from it. You really picked the wrong time to take me.'

He licked his lips and made to speak, but a noise behind him caught her attention. Victoria peered around his muscular frame and caught sight of a tiny, slim woman with blue-purple hair cut into a pixie style leaning against the door jamb. Her face was decorated in lavish make up and she had a variety of piercings. While Victoria knew she couldn't overpower the man—although her stiletto heel driven into his foot would work nicely at slowing him down—the woman's facial decorations would give Victoria an easy way to inflict pain.

But first, she needed to know if there were others around and where they were. How many were there? Were they all together or spread out? What building was she in? How many floors up, or was she below ground? How—

She grimaced; her head hurt too much to continue, but one thing she did know was that if she managed to get out of this alive, she was going to get on the phone to Mr Daven the first chance she got and *demand* she and her sisters have their security reinstated. Surely, her father wouldn't have wanted *this* to happen?

'We haven't kidnapped you,' the man said, recapturing her attention. 'I found you outside. Don't you remember *anything* about this evening?'

'You *found* me?' she scoffed. 'Was I lost?' She took a small step back as she spoke, resting her weight on her back foot, ready to drive the other into his, heel first. Once she was past the blue-haired imp, the shoes would have to come off and be used as hand weapons instead—a stiletto to the throat was almost as good as a knife.

'You were out cold—'

'Cormac saved you!' the woman interjected from her guard post. 'If he hadn't—'

'Thanks, Geri,' the man said, keeping his eyes fixed on Victoria. While she knew he was only doing so to ensure she didn't try anything, she found herself unable to look away, mesmerised by the tiny little flecks of gold hidden within their green depths. The gold shimmered and-

'I was on a date,' she blurted out as the image of a restaurant came rushing out of the fog. She'd been at a table, watching someone pouring wine into a glass. But why did she remember that?

The wine had gold leaf in it. She'd thought it pretentious. Very new money.

'That was a *date*?' the man—Cormac—asked.

'Alexi, set me up,' she replied quietly, not really considering her words as she focused on trying to force her brain to remember more.

'Alexi needs better taste in men,' Cormac told her with a shake of his head. 'It was a good job my car alarm went off—'

'Yes!' she squealed with a clap of her hands; the sound of blaring bounced around her memory. 'I set it off.' But she couldn't remember how she'd done it or how she'd got from the restaurant to said car. Her mind was filled with blank patches, not even shadowy or fuzzy images floated around. There was just... *nothing*.

'Do you know who the guy was?' Pixie-lady—no, Geri —asked.

'Ian.' Victoria tried the name, but it didn't feel quite right on her tongue, as if it was incomplete. She shook her head, trying to pull the memory of saying the man's name. It had begun with an... S! Sam, Scott...

No, she had to go further back, before the date, before she'd lost parts of her mind.

'He's not my *cup of tea,'* Alexi had told her, *which in Alexi- speak translated to fat, boring, and bald. 'But you can't afford to be*

picky. Simon's harmless—even has his own money to boot. It is new, but it means-'

'Simon.' Victoria breathed the name. 'His name was Simon.'

The clatter of footsteps rushing up a staircase distracted the imp. She turned to whatever was beyond the door of the crappy room.

'Lady Snape? Victoria?' A deep voice, one she was *very* familiar with called up the stairs. It held a hint of worry and panic under its otherwise smooth timbre. Most wouldn't notice, wouldn't hear anything but calm confidence, but she could pick it out a mile away.

It snapped her out of the spell the man in front of her was trying to put her under with his damn bewitching eyes. Damn, this guy was good. He'd almost had her there—did he use that eye trick on all his victims?

Cormac glanced back towards the doorway and while his attention was diverted, Victoria took the opportunity to make a getaway. She cursed herself for changing her stance, but she could work with it. She kicked him just below the knee, making him cry out in pain, bending forward to grab at the injury, giving her a chance to drive her elbow into his solar plexus. He grunted as the air was knocked from his lungs and he dropped to the floor on his hands and knees, gasping for breath. He wouldn't be there for long; she wasn't strong enough to really wind a man of his stature, but it would give her the time she needed to get to Marcus.

She screamed like a banshee as she deftly ran at her next target, hands up ready to make use of the rings and studs that decorated Geri's face. Her war-cry drowned out the other girl's squeal of surprise and horror at the oncoming attack, forcing Geri to back up until she hit the wall across the corridor. The woman squeezed her eyes shut, her whole face scrunching up and turning away in preparation for a smack, and Victoria wanted to laugh at the thought as she charged forward.

But before she could show the woman what she actually intended to do, someone grabbed Victoria's hands, spinning her around by her arm and into their body, wrapping her in their arms and stopping her from hurting him or anyone else.

'Lady Victoria, please,' the warm familiar voice rumbled in her ear. 'Calm yourself. You did good. I'm so proud of you, so *bloody* proud of you, Tori. You have no idea, baby girl, no idea how proud. But these aren't the ones at fault. You don't need to hurt them. God, you did so well…'

It took a few minutes, a few more whispered words of comfort, of praise, reminding her over and over that she was safe now, safe and with him again, before she felt herself melting into Marcus' warm embrace.

'Marcus,' she cried as she buried herself in the arms of the one man she knew would keep her safe: the Head of the Royal Guard, her grandfather's personal protection force. She threw her arms around his neck as she confessed, her voice small, 'Marcus, I don't know where I am…'

'It's okay, you're safe. You're safe.' Marcus repeated the words over and over until she believed him. She sagged against his body as the fight ran out of her. The feel of his hands gently rubbing her back in comfort was warm and familiar. His voice held a warmth she hadn't heard in a long time, and she instinctively nuzzled into his neck, breathing in the familiar scent of her ex-lover. The man to whom she had given her heart… before he had broken it and tossed it away.

'Victoria,' Marcus murmured in her ear, making her tremble and shiver. It had been so long since they'd really spoken, since they'd been this close to one another, and Victoria didn't want to let go. If she held on, this could be real, and they could be *them* again, a couple, two people in-

'You need to let me go. For propriety's sake, Tori.'

Propriety. The very same word he'd used four years ago when he'd said goodbye, leaving her broken, empty, and confused. When she'd sealed up her heart and vowed to never again open it to anyone.

She unwound her arms from his neck and took one final deep breath, taking his scent with her as she stepped back and looked up. He still looked as handsome as he had back then, when he was swiftly climbing the ranks of the Guard, and just seeing him so close made her breath hitch and her heart long for what it had lost. She wanted to reach out, to run her hand down his cheek, feel his smooth ebony skin under her ivory fingers before he pulled her against him and captured her mouth in his sweet, gentle kiss.

Victoria shook her head of the thought, reminding herself of what he'd done, of how much he'd hurt her. How he'd dashed her hopes and killed her dreams. How he'd never given her a real explanation of ending their engagement so quickly, leaving her confused, helpless, and utterly alone.

'What are *you* doing here?' she asked, taking a step back from him. 'Did my grandfather send you...'

She trailed off as she gazed around the tatty corridor; the paint on the walls was peeling, broken lights flickered along the ceiling, and the rusting, industrial metal stairs that led to who-knew-where didn't exactly scream safety. Yet Marcus didn't appear to be in a hurry to arrest anyone.

'Will someone *please* tell me where the hell I am and what I'm doing here!' she snapped. She turned to face the man who'd supposedly taken care of her, although why he'd needed to—shirtless, no less!—was still lost on her. 'And, why are you half dressed?'

The stranger stopped rubbing his shin to gaze down at his own naked torso before raising his eyes back to hers. He shrugged and said, 'You're at *Monty's*.'

Victoria sniffed, crossing her arms over her chest before she said, 'Never heard of it.'

'It's an all-male strip club,' Geri supplied. 'We've only just reopened under a new name. We used to be-'

'You're a stripper?' Victoria asked, interrupting the woman. Her eyes travelled over Cormac's form, finally able to appreciate his near nakedness. His torso was well-defined, his shoulders broad, his arms thick, but not overly so, and his pectorals had good definition… Hattie would call his well-toned abdomen something ridiculous… A six-pack?

If she wasn't in the situation she was in, she'd have taken a moment—probably several—to appreciate the man's perfect form and extremely handsome face, but her mind was still cloudy. She had most definitely not been here for her date.

'We weren't here…' she told them as she tried to fill in the blanks. 'How did I get here?' She was being a bossy little madam, but she didn't care. She'd woken up in a strange place, had massive gaps in her memory, and was more frightened than she'd ever been in her life. Not that she was going to confess that titbit, but she had a feeling it was showing when Cormac's face softened.

'I brought you in here after I chased that guy away, but how you got to the club's car park, I've no idea.' He shrugged and dipped his head, tucking his chin towards his chest as he mumbled his next words. 'I'm glad you did though; if you'd gone anywhere else…' Victoria saw a hint of colour tinge his cheeks as he stared intently at the floor, scuffing it with his feet.

'I—I think he drugged the wine,' she finally said, slowly and reluctantly taking her eyes away from her rescuer. 'I know I only had one glass; I remember refusing another of the stupid stuff. And I skipped dessert completely.'

'That's not like you with your sweet tooth,' Marcus said quietly.

'He was creepy.' Her words were short and crisp as she turned back to her ex, frowning. 'I remember I didn't like him from the moment I met him. Brash, loud, flashy…'

'Tell me who *he* is, Victoria,' Marcus said, his voice soft and his eyes filled with warmth and concern. 'Give me his name, and I'll handle him. Personally.'

She narrowed her eyes at the Guard, reminding herself that *he* was the one who'd walked away from her. In the last four years, they'd seen each other only during royal events she'd been forced to attend. They'd never spoken more than what was courteous, what was *appropriate* for a Lady and a Guardsman—even if he was head of the force. It had been so painful to even see the uniform the guardsmen wore, she'd declined royal protection outside of official events and had used her father's security team instead. She'd been too proud to call the royal security service up after the funeral and ask for protection when she couldn't use her father's men any longer.

She drew herself up, straightening her back and squaring her slender shoulders as she stared at the man. Marcus saw the change in her immediately, his own stance changing into something more formal. He became the formidable man he was known to be, his eyes hard and assessing as she gave him everything she knew.

'Simon. I can't remember his surname, but Alexi set us up.'

Marcus' mouth became a thin line as he clicked his fingers at the two officers behind him, making them snap to attention again.

'I'll have someone speak to Lady Alexandra *immediately*.' The moment the words were out of his mouth, one of the women quickly turned and hurried back down the stairwell. Victoria should have known his behaviour was all manipulation. Yes, this time it was for her benefit, but that was all there was to Marcus Walker.

'This has been a... weird night,' she declared, rubbing her forehead as she felt the onset of the headache returning. 'I'm going home.'

'You can't just go home, Victoria,' Marcus told her. The remaining officer behind him agreed.

'We have to take you to hospital, ma'am,' the younger woman said. 'If you were indeed drugged—'

'Are you calling me a liar?' she snapped, raising her eyes and glaring at the woman.

'No, my lady!'

'Victoria.' Marcus's voice was low, warning her she was being a bitch. She didn't care. Her head hurt, her body ached, her knees were throbbing, and she had no idea why. She was tired, she was confused, and seeing *him* standing there only added heartache to her growing list of pains. 'We also need to check you weren't sexually assaulted.'

Her hand flew to her throat at Marcus' suggestion. The thought hadn't even occurred to her. How could she have been so stupid not to think of that! She'd been out cold for goodness knew how long before she'd been found. What if the bastard had—

She felt herself sway on her feet before a strong arm encircled her waist from behind and drew her towards a firm, hard body. She leaned against it willingly, welcoming the warmth it provided and the strength it offered to protect her.

'You weren't.' It was Cormac, his deep timbre rumbling against her ear, causing a delicious shiver down her spine. Victoria looked up, and he met her gaze with those magic eyes, ensnaring her once more, and something within her knew that every word he spoke was the truth.

'When I got to you, he was sort of standing over you, as if he'd just got there himself. And, please forgive me if I screwed this up, but I asked Geri to... um...' He faulted, and Victoria's eyes strayed to his cheeks to watch the flush of colour fill them again. She had to stop herself from smiling at his bashfulness; it was endearing, cute, and honest. Not something she usually came across in a man.

'I peeked!' Geri squeaked from behind Cormac, breaking the moment.

Victoria blinked at the woman's declaration, unsure she'd heard it correctly. She frowned, turning in Cormac's arms to lean around his strong body to see her. She expected him to drop his hold on her and was pleasantly surprised when he didn't. 'I beg your pardon?'

'Nothing pervy!' the blue-haired woman hastened to add. 'I just looked, with Cormac watching-'

Cormac groaned, and dropped his chin to his chest again, his eyes screwed tight.

'Not helping, Ger.'

'It was just to make sure it was all still... there. And it was. Is! All still there. That is. Tights undisturbed. Not even a snag. Where on earth do you get them? I mean. Oh, God, I'm so sorry!'

'Do you realise-'

'Marcus.' Victoria held her hand up to stop the Guard going for the poor waif. She knew she *should* be annoyed some random woman had peeked up her skirt, but she found it hard to be angry at the girl when all she'd done was see if she needed additional help. What if she *had* woken up to find her tights around her ankles and herself violated...

God, just the thought turned her stomach.

Victoria closed her eyes to push the thought away, giving herself a moment to collect herself, but the soft squeeze of her hip and a hand gently taking hers and holding it against their chest made her peer back up at Cormac. His chest was warm, if a little slippery with baby oil, and she swore she could feel the rhythm of his heart beneath her fingers as he held her eyes with his own.

'I promise you,' he said, his voice a rich, warm rumble. It

sent another delicious shiver down her spine that was completely inappropriate for the situation but felt completely right to her body. 'He didn't get to touch you. I got there in time and I'll get the security footage from my boss to confirm it.'

That nervous little smile reappeared at the corner of his lips, making it twitch and his eyes shimmer hopefully at her. His arm around her waist tightened as if to reassure her she was safe, and Victoria felt herself lean more into him. He was handsome, brave, and strong. Any other time and she might have-

'I'll need a copy of that tape.' Marcus' voice was cold and firm as it broke the moment between them. Victoria glared at the man who met her gaze with indifference, but Victoria knew better.

'If one of your officers stays behind, I'll get Axel to find it for you.'

'Thank you,' Victoria said, calling Cormac's gaze back to hers. She smiled up at him and he returned it, and Victoria knew if he hadn't been holding her up, she'd have swooned.

'Victoria, you still need to go to the-'

'I'm not going, Marcus,' she said, reluctantly taking her eyes from Cormac's as she turned to face her ex. She should have pulled away from the man behind her, should have gently let his fingers go from hers, slowly pulled herself from his embrace. But this man had saved her, protected her, and most importantly, faced down her ex with her. She needed his strength right now.

Also, she simply didn't want him to let her go.

'You know what will happen if I go to hospital,' she continued. 'No doubt the press already knows of my presence here, and we all know they'll make up whatever reason suits them. If I also get snapped going to a bloody hospital, I'll be hauled in front of *him*, and then I have to explain all *this* to His Majesty and there's no way in hell I'm-'

She froze as she looked at the man in front of her. Her body going rigid in Cormac's hold made the man drop her hand and remove his arm, but she didn't step away from his warmth.

'You're here... He already knows, doesn't he!' She ran her hands over her head, her fingers grabbing her hair as she pulled at it and turned herself away from Marcus again. Cormac's hands reached for her, just in case, but didn't touch her, much to her disappointment. She wanted to bury herself in his arms, snuggle herself into the crook of his neck, and let him fight away all the monsters and demons that were in her life. Just as he had Simon that night.

'No, he doesn't.' Marcus shook his head vehemently. 'I intercepted the call when I heard your name on the police line. I promise he won't find out.'

'You can't make that promise,' she said, hopelessly, staring at a spot on the floor. 'He finds out bloody everything. There's no privacy in any of our lives.'

The corridor fell silent, the hum of the lights above the only sound as four pairs of eyes focused on her. Her shoulders finally slumped as the fight completely left her and she gave in.

'He's going to find out, so let's just go and get this over with.' She knew her voice was filled with sad defeat.

'Victoria, perhaps-'

'Just give me a moment, okay, Marcus?'

She felt the man hesitate, knew he wanted to say something more, reach out or do something. But instead, she heard him turn around, the sound of his feet on the stairs telling of his retreat, the secondary officer following in haste after him.

'Will you be okay?' Cormac asked when their footsteps had disappeared and the sound of a heavy door at the bottom of the stairwell closed behind them. Victoria shrugged, her eyes still on the floor. From the corner of her vision, she saw his hand reach out and a single finger carefully tipped her chin up.

He was shirtless, glistening with baby oil, and probably at least five years her junior; it was utterly preposterous, but he looked every inch the fairy tale prince, ready to fight dragons and demons to save his princess. She groaned and leaned forward, resting her head on his chest, uncaring what the oil would do to her hair. He immediately wrapped his arms around her and pulled her tight into a hug.

It was completely surreal; this man was a stranger, a complete and utter stranger, but he'd fought off her attacker, brought her to safety, and stood at her side against Marcus. She felt far safer with him than anyone else in the world in that moment, and being his in arms just felt *right*.

'I will be,' she muttered against him. 'Not the first time something like this has happened, probably won't be the last.'

She felt his body tense against her. 'Really? That bad?'

'Eh.' She shrugged. 'Comes with the territory of being royalty.' She gave herself one moment, savouring the warmth he provided, before she pulled away and stepped back. 'Too bad I can't have a handsome prince around every corner to rescue me,' she said giving him a sad smile. 'Sorry about kicking you.'

'Well, if you ever need rescuing again, just give me a call. I'll even let you kick me in the shin again.' He gave her a wink. She smiled, but it didn't reach her eyes and by the slight downturn of his delectable mouth, he knew it. 'Seriously, though, if you do ever need anything—not that there's much a simple stripper can give you,' he chuckled. 'Except a lap dance—'

He froze at his words and she heard Geri groan from where she'd hidden herself in the kitchen to give them their privacy. His cheeks flamed bright red, and Victoria noted the colour extended to the tops of his ears. She laughed, properly and heartily for what felt the first time in a long time.

'I didn't mean—'

'Cormac…?' She waited for him to provide his full name for her, but Cormac just stared at her expectantly.

'Blake!' Geri pipped up, still hidden around her corner.

'Cormac Blake,' she said, stepping up to the flushed man and cupping his cheek in the palm of her hand so he'd gaze at her. 'Never sell yourself short. I'm sure that you are a wonderful, talented young man who has much to offer *any* woman. Including Ladies of the Realm.' She gently guided his head downward and placed a kiss upon his forehead—not exactly where she wanted to put it.

'And maybe'—she stepped away and started towards the stairs—'I'll take you up on the lap dance one day.'

∽

Cormac watched Victoria's swaying hips as she began her descent down the dimly lit steps. The low thrum of arousal he'd been feeling since she'd woken up and stuck that plump, kissable lip out in a pout, intensified, wiping out the ache in his side from where she'd elbowed him. He shifted his stance, wincing slightly and hoped it looked more like he was still in pain, than trying to hide his interested cock in the painfully tight trousers of the uniform he wore when waiting on tables rather than dancing on stage.

But he paused mid-shift, suddenly uncaring who saw him sporting a semi, when Victoria turned at the landing to the next set of stairs and lifted her gaze to his. Her caramel eyes, catching a strip of light perfectly, made him forget everything else in that moment.

Cormac finally understood, as they gazed at one another, what people meant by time seeming to stop. The air seemed to still, sound faded away, and any other care or worry in the world disappeared as they peered into each other's souls.

A second. That was all it was. One second. The tiniest

fraction of his lifetime. A measure so small, so insignificant that he wasted so many of them daily. A blink of an eye. A huff of breath. A signature on a document. All important things one could do in such a short space of time, yet they all paled in comparison to how he felt in that moment.

'You okay there?' Geri asked, finally stepping out from her hiding place. He jumped at the interruption and blinked away whatever look was on his face—he didn't even want to contemplate what he'd looked like.

It was unsettling, unnerving to feel so sucker punched from just a *look*. But that was exactly how he felt as he watched Victoria lower her eyes as she continued her descent.

'Cormac?'

'Yeah. Yes?' he said as he ran his hand down his suddenly tired face while he tried to make sense of everything that had happened this evening. That was what was making him disorientated; the excitement, the drama, not the woman he was watching disappearing from his life. The woman he'd held in his arms, who he hadn't wanted to let go the moment she turned into him. Who'd made his stomach drop when he'd thought she was going to kiss him, and the rise of disappointment he'd felt when her lips brushed his forehead instead.

No, it had absolutely *nothing* to do with Lady Victoria Snape.

'What a night,' Geri said, heading back into the kitchen.

'You said it,' Cormac agreed as he slowly turned away, and tried to push the thought of his princess from his mind. But her gaze at him, those beautiful caramel eyes framed by long dark lashes, had seared itself into his soul. He knew he'd be dreaming of those eyes for many nights to come, picturing that pouting mouth when alone in the shower, and wondering, if he'd just lifted his head and caught her lips with his, what she'd taste like as he lay in bed, alone.

Cormac groaned as he stepped into the kitchen and saw the grin on Geri's face. Even if he could forget his princess, there was no way Geri was going to let him forget *anything*. Nor would any of the guys downstairs the moment they heard about it... from the little imp.

CHAPTER FOUR

Victoria hurriedly climbed into the back of one of the royal cars when a camera flash popped. She cursed as she settled into her seat and glared at Marcus as he climbed in beside her, closing the door and hiding them away from the world for the time being.

'I told you this would happen,' she snarled as the driver pulled away from the back of the club. She stared angrily through the dark tinted windows, knowing whoever was lurking out there couldn't see her, but hoping she could somehow curse them for their callous invasion of her life.

For a brief moment, she wondered if they'd have helped her, if they'd been the ones to come across her being attacked by Simon, or if they would have just snapped away as he'd done whatever he'd had planned? She threw that thought away as fast as it came; he hadn't managed to do anything to her, and she knew that by the morning, Marcus would have located the evil bastard and had him thrown in the Broken Hill, where traitors had been held and tried for centuries.

By the afternoon, she imagined the man next to her would have interrogated her attacker, received a file full of evidence against him and his co-conspirators, and by this time tomorrow night they'd all be rounded up and joining the man in Avalone's highest security prison.

'All they got was you coming out of the back of a club. Nothing unusual there—at least not lately.' Marcus' voice was filled with disdain as he spoke of her recent dating spree as she tried to find a husband before her next birthday. The once rarely seen Lady Snape stepping out almost nightly with a different man on her arm had been the discussion and headline of many a magazine, gossip blog, and entertainment show over the last three months as they puzzled over the sudden change in her actions. It was why she knew there'd be someone waiting to take her picture.

Had they seen Simon's attack on her? Had they followed her as she tried to escape from the man, recording her plight ready to sell to the highest bidder? She shuddered at the thought.

Before that night, the most vicious rumour they'd concocted was that her father had forbidden her to date and now that he was six feet under, Victoria was free to sow her royal oats wherever she pleased. But now…

She turned and narrowed her eyes at the guardsman. 'An all-male *strip* club, Marcus,' she reminded him. '*And* you know they're going to follow us. They'll get me going from such a place to a hospital. Who knows what they'll come up with to explain *that?*'

The man at her side sighed. 'Victoria, we—'

'No, you don't get to be so informal anymore!' She snapped, holding her finger up to him. She knew she was being a bitch, but she didn't care. She was angry and scared over what had happened and he was part of the reason. 'You will address me accordingly. As fitting for *propriety's sake.*'

'Yes. My lady,' the Guard growled.

It was the first time she'd stood her ground against him.

Usually, she diverted her gaze from him whenever they were together at events and tried to stay as far from him as she could, being polite and emotionally distant when she couldn't. She'd never spoken down to him, never made him feel the subject he was to her, but she was feeling raw and off kilter. He'd stormed to the rescue, just as he had ten years ago during another kidnapping attempt, and acted hot and cold. He was playing with her heart and it wasn't fair.

He'd broken her without explaining why, leaving her with unanswered questions and always wondering if it was something *she'd* done or if he had just been weak enough to allow her grandfather to buy him off as the rumours had suggested.

She ground her teeth at the thought that if he hadn't walked away, she wouldn't be in the situation she was now. They'd have been married for years, probably would have had a child or two, and she'd have received every penny of her inheritance she was entitled to the moment her father had died.

She turned her attention to the twinkling beauty of the capital sliding by as they quickly and quietly crept through the sparkling streets towards whichever hospital Marcus had deemed fit.

This was all his fault.

And her father's.

She felt her fingers curl in on themselves, her nails digging into the palms of her hands as she realised it was really her father who had put her in the position she'd been in tonight, by setting such stupid stipulations in his will for each of his daughters.

He'd made her vulnerable, made her dependent on someone else with his ridiculous conditions, and she had no idea why he'd done it.

While her father had always been a level-headed, deeply focused businessman, she'd always reasoned he had to have had a romantic streak within him. He'd wooed her seventeen-year-old mother and married her on her eighteenth birthday… Sure, he'd been fifteen years her senior and most people felt it creepy that such an older man had fallen for a woman so young, but it must have been love at first sight for him as much as it was for her mother; why else would he go against the King of Avalone and incur his wrath?

At first, she'd reasoned that was why he'd put the marriage requirement in there; he wanted his daughters to find love, to begin families so they could know the joy he had with their mother, but now…

Now, she realised he was simply forcing her to prostrate herself at the feet of men to survive. She wasn't a weak, feeble little thing, yet tonight she'd felt exactly that. Waking in a strange place with no knowledge of how she'd got there…

Tonight could have ended much worse than it had; she could have been kidnapped, raped, or killed. Hell, she could have endured all three!

And the sad thing was, she knew she would have to potentially put herself back into such situations again, as soon as she could. She had to have a husband, else she'd lose it all and be beholden to her grandfather, and she'd rather live out the rest of her days in Broken Hill than face such a future.

Her mind reeled at the thought. She felt like a prostitute, having to pimp herself out to claim what was rightfully hers. She felt dirty, unwanted, as if she was merely an empty vessel without a man to complete her.

But, she considered, as rain began to spatter against her window, what if she turned the tables? What if *she* were the one controlling how she got her part of the family fortune?

She glanced out of the corner of her eye towards where Marcus sat quietly, tapping away on his tablet, no doubt directing a full investigation into her date that evening. She considered him for a moment. They knew each other…

She quickly shook her head of the thought. Too much history between them, too much unsaid that should have been said so long ago.

She sighed, causing Marcus to momentarily glance her way before turning back to whatever it was he was reading.

She needed someone outside of the royal world, so they weren't influenced by her grandfather. Someone she could make an offer they could never refuse. Someone she could trust to look out for her if need be. Someone brave enough to stand by her side against everyone else.

She snorted at the idea she was looking for Prince-bloody-Charming. If such a man had ever existed, then surely-

She sat up straight as the perfect thought struck her.

'Marcus…' She said his name slowly as a plan began to form in her mind.

'Yes, Lady Snape?' From her peripheral vision, she saw him raise his head to her again.

'I need to know everything you can find out about Cormac…' She searched her memory. 'Cormac Blake. And I mean *everything*. As soon as possible.'

'Victoria, what the hell is going on?' She merely raised her brow at his frustrated tone. When she refused to answer, he huffed in annoyance and turned back to his device, his finger forcefully pressing the screen as he no doubt began his search on Cormac.

Knowing she'd won that round, Victoria sank back into her seat, finally feeling the tension she'd been carrying for months ease somewhat from her shoulders. She pulled her phone from her bag—discovered by one of Marcus' lesser officers—and typed out a message to Pippa telling her she'd be back later than planned.

Even the flash of a camera as she climbed out of the car,

the hospital clear behind her, didn't stop the bounce in her step as she entered the building to begin what would no doubt be another humiliating round of tests.

She was going to get her inheritance—she just had to buy it first.

CHAPTER FIVE

The sun streamed in through the tiny window of the compact kitchen, bathing Cormac Blake in its warm beam. He took a deep breath of hot, freshly cooked breakfast, before picking up the thick slice of well-buttered toast and dipping it into his fried eggs to pop the gooey, golden centre. He bit a chunk from the slice, then rested it on his plate and wiped his fingers against his trouser legs.

He reached out for the still folded paper on the table at the top of his plate, completing his morning ritual. He'd read the paper while eating, then he'd make a start on the daily slog. But first, bacon...

He flipped the paper open with one hand as he snagged a piece of the crispy meat from his plate with the other, folding it into his mouth and moaning shamelessly as its flavour bloomed over his tongue. When he opened his eyes from what could only be described as a food orgasm, he scanned the front-page story and groaned. There was a full-page spread about Lady Victoria Snape leaving *Monty's* via the staff entrance with a full royal protection unit, including the Head of the Royal Guard.

His eyes greedily read the story as it detailed how the

distinguished man at her side, Marcus Walker, was her exboyfriend, although rumours still suggested he was actually her *ex-fiancé*. Cormac briefly wondered if it was true, before mentally shrugging and reading on for anything involving the truth of the night.

Nothing was mentioned about the attack on her, of his rescue, or her date earlier that night, although, speculation was rife about why she'd been taken straight from the strip club to the hospital. He snorted as he read the line about her requiring the morning-after pill after being caught *in flagrante* with one of the strippers.

I wouldn't mind being caught with my pants down with her, he thought as he reached for his coffee, taking in the profile of the cool and composed Lady Snape as she stood at the side of the car staring up at the hospital. He'd always had a thing for older ladies, and especially those *way* out of his league.

He took another sip of his coffee as he turned the page but cursed up a storm as he missed his lip and the scalding hot liquid splashed in his lap.

'Son of a—'

'Don't say that word,' James, Cormac's six-year-old brother, chastised as he came into the kitchen, yawning. The kid, far too skinny for his age, fell into the chair next to Cormac's, propped his elbow on the table and rested his head on his hand as he stared at his big brother through sleepy eyes. 'Mum would give you a crack if she heard you.'

And wasn't that the truth? Every time Cormac had uttered a word of profanity in her presence, he'd felt the palm of her hand across the back of his head. And with the mouth he'd had growing up, he was surprised he didn't have brain damage.

Not that James really knew that fact; he'd been a bit of surprise to his parents when they'd conceived. They'd been preparing to see their then-only child headed off for university when their mother had discovered she was pregnant again. James had been less than a week old when their parents had died in a car accident on their way home from hospital after his birth, and Cormac had suddenly become his guardian. However, he had entertained his brother enough with stories of them over the past few years for it to feel as if James knew their parents. It was one of only two things Cormac could say he was proud of; the other was James himself.

He watched as his brother grabbed his fork and speared the sausage on his plate. He took a hearty bite, chomping away as he propped a book open on the table so he could practise his reading before school. Cormac smiled fondly as James frowned at a word and tried to mouth it, showing the masticated meat inside—the kid had worse table manners than he did, and that was saying something.

'Here,' Cormac said, picking up his plate and pushing his two sausages onto James' own. 'Eat up. Growing boys need their breakfasts. And use your knife.' The young boy huffed before he rubbed his eyes tiredly.

'You up late?' Cormac asked, his mouth full of bacon as he gauged his brother. James nodded, his nose wrinkling in distaste at Cormac's lack of manners—Pot. Kettle. Black.—and it only made Cormac shove another piece of bacon past his lips before he asked, 'Homework or that damn PlayStation?'

James quickly dropped his gaze and answered with a mumbled, *Homework*. Cormac snorted. He was starting to regret giving his brother the ageing console he'd had since *he* was a kid. The kids in James' class all had shiny, fancy *new* gaming machines and flat panel TVs, and James had come home asking if he could have one for Christmas. It was the first time his little brother had asked for anything and Cormac had felt guilty he couldn't afford one. He'd found the PlayStation 2 in a box of his old junk and hooked it up to the small twenty-one-inch tube TV he still held on to, even if one side of the screen had turned yellow.

'You know, if you don't get your eight hours, you're going to stay that short,' Cormac warned, dipping his toast in his egg again before shoving the slice in his mouth. He stood up, pushing what was left on his plate onto his brother's, telling James to finish the lot before he headed into the living room.

He sighed as he began the job of stripping the sheets from the sofa-bed and folding the couch away again. He dumped the sheets in the tiny cupboard their landlord had mockingly dubbed a *utility room* and headed to the one bedroom the flat held; James'.

'I can do it!' he heard his brother protest quickly when the kid realised where he was going. But James was too late. Cormac had already seen the bed stripped and the sheets bundled into the corner. A towel over the bare mattress told him his little brother had had another nightmare. Cormac ran a hand over his face, rubbing at his stubble-covered jaw as James ran through the door, begging his brother not to look.

'I'm sorry,' James whispered, skidding to a stop within the door frame. 'I didn't mean to.' His young voice filled with shame as he lowered his head made Cormac want to cry.

Instead, he turned to his little brother, his large hand covering James' shoulder and gave it a comforting squeeze. 'Happens to the best of us,' he said, and if his voice was a little gruffer than usual, James didn't comment.

Cormac grabbed the towel from the bed and gathered the soiled sheets quickly, humming a happy tune as he went, trying to help his brother relax over the matter. He wished he could figure out what the hell was causing James to have the nightmares; he'd tried to talk to him about them, but the kid clammed up the moment he asked.

'Postman's here!' James called out as Cormac stuffed the sheets into the washing machine. He shut the machine's door just as the large pack of mail was thrust through the letterbox. James grabbed what Cormac knew consisted only of bills and ran past him back into the kitchen. Cormac headed back into the small living room and sat on the old, worn-out sofa for a moment, rubbing his fingers over his tired eyes as he took a second to compose himself.

The rates—gas, electric, and water—were due for renewal this month and he begged whatever entity was out there in the cosmos that they wouldn't have increased too much. He was already two months behind on the rent.

He slapped his hands on his knees before he stood up and headed back to the kitchen. He gathered the mail that had been haphazardly strewn across the table and tore the envelopes open, his heart sinking with each new bill. Gas, up. Water, up. Electricity… surprise, surprise, up. *Way* up.

Even his car insurance was up another five crowns a year and he wasn't even sure it was worth that much. He tried to do the maths, adding together the totals and dividing the answer by twelve, but the smashing of a glass tore him away from his calculations.

'I'm sorry,' James whispered, standing at the side of the table, his plate in one hand and the remnants of a glass at his feet. His little brother looked up at him with his big hazel eyes, wide with fright and worry. Cormac fell back against the counter and rubbed his left eye, dragging his hand down his cheek as he tried to remain composed. At least the glass had been empty.

'It's okay, accidents happen. But you know you're not supposed to carry it like that—you take the plate, *then* the glass.'

'I know,' James said, lowering his head. 'I just wanted to help.'

'I get it,' Cormac said, stepping towards him. 'But we have rules to stop this kind of thing from happening.' He carefully leaned over the shattered glass and heaved his brother up in the air. He turned and put him down on the carpet in the hallway.

'Go and get ready for school,' he said. 'I'll sort out this mess.'

He heard the soft pitter-patter of his brother's feet run off down the hallway as he turned back to the kitchen, his eyes drifting to the stack of bills on the table; at least broken glass was an easy fix.

∼

'Hey, shrimp!'

James spun around, his smile beaming.

The little guy ran towards Cormac, his tiny blazer flapping around his waist where he'd tied it. Cormac bent down, arms out, and gathered James into a hug as the boy flung himself at him.

'How was school?' Cormac asked and smiled as James launched into a tale of his day in minute detail as only a child could. Cormac nodded and made the right sounds at the right time to show he was listening, but he also had a million other things to think about for when they got home.

The club's revamp had meant the on-site gym had been removed, and they'd all been given priority membership at some swanky gym, but it was thirty minutes in the wrong direction. With the contractual three hours a day he had to spend there to keep his body in tip-top shape, it basically meant he was always rushing to and from the school with barely enough time for one or two errands after his workout session. Everything else had to fit in between taking James home and heading off to work.

'—and the blood was so red and thick, and Maria screamed! Miss Spencer had to—'

'Whoa, wait, what?' Cormac asked, his head snapping up as he strapped James into his booster seat at the back of the car. James huffed and folded his arms across his chest; his tiny scowl made Cormac want to laugh, but he kept his face as neutral as possible so he could find out if someone had been murdered or maimed in the classroom and prayed James hadn't been the culprit. 'Who was bleeding?'

'No one,' James said with a put-upon sigh and a shake of his head. Cormac raised a brow at his reaction, wondering where the hell his kid brother was getting such an attitude. 'Miss Spencer cut up a pig's heart and it *oozed*...' James' eyes went wide as he said 'oozed' and Cormac couldn't help a relieved puff of breath escaping.

'That's a new word for you,' he said as he settled into the driver's seat directly in front of James. He pushed his concerns away that they were already dissecting things at six years old as he tried to focus on James' tale. He knew his brother was exceptionally clever and already needed pushing academically, but surely there should be some boundaries.

'Miss Spencer said it,' James informed him matter-of-factly before turning his attention out of the window, his small hands pressing against the glass as he watched out for his friends to wave goodbye to them.

When they got back to the flat, Cormac told James to go do his homework.

'But Corrie—'

'Don't *but Corrie* me,' he said, setting down the two bags of food he'd bought before he picked up James. James heaved his books from his little backpack and spread them over the available space on the small kitchen table. Cormac hummed under his breath as he unpacked the fresh fruit and vegetables; they'd been in the reduced counter, so they'd have to be used up that night or tomorrow. He pushed a banana towards James, who was copying words carefully with a pencil into his practice book. James could read at an academy level and his maths skills were almost there too, but smarts clearly didn't go with fine motor skills; his handwriting was barely legible—to anyone but James.

'Eat your snack, I'm going to cook us some stir-fry tonight.'

'Do you have to?' Cormac rolled his eyes at his brother's pouting tone. James wasn't fond of cabbage and carrots, but Cormac insisted the kid eat his vegetables.

'I got steak to go in it this time.' That perked James right up. He didn't say it had been over half off, was just about to turn, and was no way near big enough for the two of them. He'd just make sure he cooked it well, and that James got the lion's share.

He put the ingredients he'd use that evening to one side as he shoved the rest of the food away, once more humming to himself, wiggling his hips slightly, trying to subtly practice for that evening. His mind drifted to Lady Victoria from the night before. He wondered if she was okay and if they'd found anything at the hospital. He wished there was someone he could call to find out, just as a concerned citizen, of course, but didn't want to cause any more hassle for the minor royal. From what he'd overheard between her and that Guardsman, the grass wasn't always greener on the other side.

Although, he might take the risk for a bit of financial stability for a while.

'Why are you looking for studios?' James' voice interrupted Cormac's musing.

'Say again, buddy?' He turned to glance over his shoulder as he began heating the pan. He cursed under his breath as he saw James pulling the newspaper towards him, eyeing the circled lets he thought they could afford if he had to give up this place.

'Are you going to record a song?' James turned surprised yet impressed eyes up at him. Cormac laughed at the comment.

'Dude, you know I can't even whistle in tune, never mind hold a note.' James' surprised face scrunched up at the thought of his brother trying to sing. 'Yeah, exactly.' Cormac added, pointing at him with the spatula.

'So why are you looking at them?'

Cormac sighed as he poured the vegetables into the smoking pan. He hadn't wanted to tell James about the possibility of moving until it went from potential to necessary.

'A studio is also what people use to describe a small flat,' Cormac finally answered, trying to keep his voice upbeat.

'Smaller than here?' Cormac cringed at the wonder in his brother's voice. James was right to be surprised, they barely had enough room in this place as it was.

'Yeah, a studio is just one big room with everything in it.'

'Even the bathroom! Ew, I don't want you to see me when I have to—'

'The bathroom is separate,' Cormac said, cutting off James before he got to his unnecessary point. He'd stopped wiping the kid's backside last year and since then, his brother had been adamant on privacy. Not knowing many other parents well enough to ask, Cormac wasn't sure if it was normal or not, but it didn't seem to be causing any issues other than having to wait for his brother sometimes to get out of the damn tiny shower room that had been advertised as a family sized bathroom.

Cormac added the noodles and gave the pan a few flicks of his wrist. He could practically hear the wheels turning in James' head and braced himself for the inevitable question he knew would come.

'So, the kitchen, living room, and bedroom are all together? We'd sleep in the same room?' he asked quietly. Cormac figured James was worried he wouldn't be able to hide when he had an accident anymore—not that the kid could anyway.

'Yeah, I thought we might get bunk beds.' He knew *that*

would distract James from whatever dark thoughts were floating through his tiny head. Cormac was sure he could probably find a set going for free or for as few slivers as possible if he really looked. Maybe he could get one of those ones with a larger bottom bunk and they could use that as a sofa to save on space.

'Really?' Cormac glanced over his shoulder as he heard the boy pushing away his homework, suddenly interested in the idea. The excitement in James' eyes soothed the small ache in Cormac's chest at once more not being good enough for his brother. 'Could I get the top bunk?'

Cormac managed a laugh and a *sure* before he refocused on the meal, pushing to one side the bitter thought of how in a few years, James was going to hate the lack of privacy he'd have. After all, it was *his* one bugbear of their current situation. If they moved, he'd have to sneak moments of pleasure in the shower or in the backseat of his car behind the club when he could. So, what if he didn't have a relationship for another twelve years, until James went off to university? Eighteen years alone was a small price to pay to keep them together, to keep James with him. His parents would be proud of that, right?

He kept that thought in his head as James chatted away, happily munching on the steak and trying to avoid the vegetables. If he noticed Cormac had little meat, he didn't comment.

After they tidied away, and Cormac had done a dozen or so household jobs while James finally finished his written homework, the two retreated to the living room. James automatically switched on the PlayStation 2 and sat in front of the television. Cormac rolled his eyes in fond exasperation and settled down on the couch with another outdated textbook he'd picked up on the cheap in one of the charity shops he'd driven past that day; mathematics had been one of his choices when he'd applied to universities before their parents had been taken from them.

He cast a glance over towards the small bookshelf that housed the few books they had. Most were James' but the thicker ones on the bottom shelf were what Cormac immersed himself in when he had the chance. Law, economics, chemistry, biology, and physics were a few that sat there, mostly collecting dust. He had hopes that if James continued to develop the way he was, one day soon he'd be picking up those tomes to have a glance through himself. Cormac dreamt of James getting selected for the Guildford University Gifted Programme, one that ran every four years for the brightest teenage minds across the nation.

That thought made Cormac smile for several reasons. One it would open so many doors for his brother. Graduates of the programme went on to be leaders of industry, ambassadors of nations, or Nobel prize winners. And two, it was all expenses paid! While all universities in Avalone were free to attend, it was living costs that killed most people's chances. James would graduate without debt and with job offers from all over the globe… And those twelve lonely years might only turn out to be seven or eight.

Cormac made a note to speak to Miss Spencer tomorrow and see what else Cormac could do to help James' chances of gaining consideration for the programme.

'Corrie, why don't we have any money?' James asked, his voice casual as he continued playing his game. Cormac blinked at the question, surprised by its bluntness as much as its unexpectedness.

'What makes you think we don't have any money?' he asked, marking his page with a bookmark before slowly closing his book.

'Kenny in class said we should have loads of money because our parents are dead. But we live in a crappy flat in a bad part of town.' Cormac ignored James' use of the word *crappy* as he imagined himself strangling Kenny if he ever got hold of the little shit.

'And where did Kenny get that idea from?' He knew damn well where the kid got the idea; his parents were loaded and while they were polite to Cormac's face whenever he came across them in the playground, they probably sneered down their nose at him the moment his back was turned. Hell, they rolled up with a new car every few months—*fancying a change*—when Cormac could barely scrape together the funds for much-needed car repairs.

'He said his parents just got an—' he paused to find the word he was looking for. 'Kenny said an en-terrace, but it's not a word I know.'

'That's because Kenny's stupid. He means an inheritance.'

'Oh, right. I know *that* word.'

Of course he did, Cormac shook his head fondly, as James nodded his enthusiastically at his own understanding. However, his young eyes stayed rigorously fixed to the screen as his character ran around whatever deserted building it featured. 'His granddad died a few months ago and today he said that his dad said they're going to build a pool in their back garden. *And* his dad said that Kenny gets some money so he can buy himself a brand-new bike. Why didn't I get a bike when our mum and dad died?'

Cormac blinked at the rapid-fire information his brother dumped on him, trying to ignore the guilt twisting deep down in his stomach. He thought he had a few more years before he'd have to start answering these types of questions, owning up to his mistakes in handling their own small estate. How could he explain to a six-year-old their parents *had* left them a nice house and *almost* enough money to pay off the mortgage, but Cormac, in his youthful naïvety of thinking he knew the world at only eighteen, hadn't listened to the risks of investments, and lost the lot on a couple of bad deals.

Because of his stupidity, his little brother would never

know what it was like to have a proper home. At least not until he could afford one of his own.

'Not everybody gets an inheritance, James, not everyone is that lucky.' His voice was low and sombre, and he hoped James didn't question why. Or at least if James thought his voice was strange, that perhaps it was because he was delivering bad news rather than barefaced lies.

Cormac's stomach turned at the thought of lying to his brother, but he promised himself that he'd tell him when the time was right… In a few years. His eyes drifted of their own volition to the small table where the bills sat, and he prayed that he'd at least get that chance, that he wouldn't lose James into the foster system.

Oh, was all James said as he carried on pressing buttons on the console's pad, killing the bad guys he was fighting against. Cormac wished all conversations with the little guy could go that easily, that James would always readily accept everything Cormac told him, and that all his lies of things getting better, of their lives turning around, would come true.

'So, weren't our parents rich then?' James asked before holding the console pad up towards the TV as his fingers danced over the buttons quickly, as if somehow the controller would work better.

'They certainly didn't have a pool in their back garden,' Cormac said, opening his textbook again.

'I wish we'd got an inheritance,' James said after a few moments of silence. 'Then we wouldn't have to look at studios.'

The equations on the page blurred as Cormac's eyes filled with tears. The heavy feeling inside his chest twisted and rose into his throat, threatening to spew out into a sob as the innocent words that James spoke punched him in the stomach, and hurt Cormac in ways he didn't know he could.

He brushed the tears away quickly with his thumbs and

coughed to clear his throat of the ball that seemed to sit heavily within it. When he felt he could, Cormac opened his mouth to finally answer his brother, but was saved by the knock on the door and James' instant groan.

'Son of a—'

'James!' Cormac watched as he dropped the console's pad and crossed his arms over his chest, frowning at the telling off he knew was coming. Cormac forwent the argument they'd end up having if he bothered—*but* you *say it all the time*—and closed his book again before heaving himself off the sofa.

He really was going to have to stop using profanity around James. He certainly didn't want to get dragged into school to talk about his baby brother's language.

Cormac opened the front door, smile already on his face to welcome Mrs Battersea, pointing in the direction of the living room. He heard her greet his brother, and James' reluctant *hello*, the TV being switched off and books being dragged out again, and bit back the laugh that wanted to bubble out.

At least for now, he could be a good guy for an hour each night in his brother's eyes, even if one day that could all be ripped away from him.

CHAPTER SIX

'...Then you have Malcolm on the fifteenth, Kevin on the twentieth, Jeremy on the twenty-seventh, Franklin in the afternoon of the thirty-first, Timothy that same night at...'

Victoria sighed and rubbed a hand over her face as she rested her elbows on the large ornate desk of her office.

'Kirstie stop,' she said quietly, cupping her face in her hands and staring forlornly at her private secretary. Kirstie looked back at her, and having worked together for so long, words didn't need to be spoken between them.

'I'll cancel them all,' Kirstie said, drawing thick black lines through each name as she turned the pages of the diary. 'What's the new plan? Or do you just need time after the other night? Maybe if we speak to Mr Daven and explain what happened...'

Victoria sat back in her seat and turned around as she released another long breath from the side of her mouth. She peered out of the large floor-to-ceiling windows and watched the gardeners in the near distance, cutting and shaping the topiary into the uniform shapes she knew adorned all the gardens at every royal residence across the country. From the outside, everything had to be exactly the same, perfect in every way, just the way the King wanted it on the off-chance he'd drop by unexpectedly. Victoria prayed he continued his tradition of never visiting *her* and counted down the days until she gained her freedom—or became beholden to her grandfather forever.

Kirstie was still talking, but Victoria wasn't listening. Her mind kept drifting to the file in the bottom drawer of her desk, calling to her like a siren to a sailor, luring her to her possible demise.

Marcus hadn't taken any time in getting the report on Cormac Blake to her. It had taken only three days for him to collate everything on her rescuer, and while he was only second to her grandfather in terms of national security access, that was quick even for him.

'Don't give me that look,' he'd told her when he'd dropped it off the day before. 'That man was both the easiest and yet most difficult subject I've ever had to look into.'

Victoria hadn't believed it until she'd sat down with the file and rifled through it. All the basics were there: name, address, date of birth, school attended and his grades, his employment history, tax records, family details, and so on, but there was little else. Marcus had had him staked out for those three days, trying to explain some of the information he'd come across, but the few pictures they had of him were simple, mundane things such as working out at the gym— okay she'd enjoyed *those* images—picking up groceries, collecting his brother, and heading off to work… and that was apparently a typical day for the twenty-four-year-old.

Victoria wasn't the cleverest person in the world, but she saw what Marcus meant right away. Today, almost anyone could find out anything about anyone. Digital fingerprints were left all over the internet, leaving trails back to you regardless of how careful you were—it was why she used the royal phone network. But Cormac Blake had drawn a complete blank to the cyber-security arm of the Avalonian Guard. He had no social media accounts, no mobile phone contracts, no internet at home, no GPS device in his car... The team wasn't even sure he'd ever been on a computer—although his library card did have *IT User* assigned to it.

'...and if the public found out the truth...'

Victoria gnawed on her lower lip as she considered her options. Regardless of what truth Kirstie was talking about, the reality was she *had* to get married. She could do that either by hoping one of her dates would work out *or* she could take matters into her own hands as she'd considered in her pique of anger and humiliation five nights ago.

Either way, in less than twelve weeks, her future would be set. Either she found a man and married him, or she handed herself over to the King, who—and of this she was certain—would have her married off to a foreign prince before the year was out.

And as soon as she was wed, Alistair would be next. The only cousin she liked was going to hate her, no matter what she did. Although he'd probably take more pity on her if she were sold off by their grandfather.

As angry as she'd been at her father the other night, looking back, he had always offered her a way out. Every year on her birthday he'd offer to buy her an apartment, a house, an estate, even a yacht if that was what she wanted, if she'd just break away from the ties of the Royal Family and relinquish the role she'd felt obliged to undertake after her mother's death. But she'd always said no, always resisted, holding onto the ties of the family her mother came from, as if Victoria could somehow hold on to part of her in doing so. But now, Victoria realised, there was nothing of her mother within them.

While her mother had a been a kind and wonderful woman, the Royal Family were, well, *royal*. They'd never embraced her. Hell, they never embraced each other, and watching her sisters at their grandfather's birthday celebrations, being ignored by the lot—and Hattie ignoring her too—it had finally hit home why her mother had tried to escape them so many years ago.

Hindsight was a wonderful thing; if her father was here to ask her if she wanted out right now, her answer would be the opposite of every other she'd given in the past. She'd beg for a small country pile, nothing too ostentatious, something that needed no more than three or four staff members, rather than the dozens they had here at Renfrew. Somewhere she could hide away from the press and her relatives, somewhere her sisters could retreat to if they needed… Somewhere she could call *home*.

Perhaps this was the real reason her father had put in the stupid clause. A last-ditch attempt to get her out of the clutches of the Royal Family. She was just sorry it had taken her father's death for her to see what she needed to do. What the four of them needed.

While the other three didn't have any royal obligations—which annoyed Alexi to no end—without their inheritance, they'd still have to rely on their royal relatives if something went wrong. Pippa and Hattie could protest all they wanted, could scream at the top of their voices that they were independent and had no obligations due to their own income, but it would only take a financial crash for both of them to be out of jobs, tied to the world's economy as they were. Avalone's own financial economy may be tied to the gold standard still, unlike those in dollar-standard countries, but it would only take the price of gold to suddenly drop overnight for them to be wiped out.

Or a scandal. After all, everyone loved a good scandal, especially when it involved a member of royalty.

But even if the price of gold fell, it was better to have some gold than none. And if she had her father's gold, she'd have her freedom from any royal burden.

'It's going to take too long. I don't have the time,' Victoria said as she turned herself back around to face Kirstie. She had no idea how to approach what she wanted to suggest. Her secretary was going to think her insane. 'Do you remember my father's favourite saying?' Victoria asked as she reached down to open the bottom drawer. 'That if *you* can't make it happen, *pay* someone else to make it happen?' She plucked the file from the drawer and carefully placed it on the desk in front of her, her hands carefully folded over it as she prepared herself for the reaction she was going to get.

'I think I remember him saying that once or twice,' Kirstie said absently, as she continued to make her diary corrections.

Victoria wanted to laugh; it was what he said every time he hit a hurdle.

'What if I *hired* someone to be my husband?' Victoria held her breath as she watched Kirstie process her words. Her secretary's pen stilled, her head lifted minutely as she raised her dark eyes to meet Victoria's.

'I *beg* your pardon?'

'No, no, hear me out,' Victoria quickly pleaded 'We don't have time for me to meet somebody, fall in love, trust them enough to be able to tell them about the situation, and get married. *And* to pull it all off not only in front of my family but the world too.

'So, what if I *hired* someone who knew the situation, was bound by a non-disclosure agreement, and was bought and paid for to be my husband? They'd know the situation, they'd agree to it all, and I'd have everything contractually tied up so the world would never find out. I'd get my money, they'd get a pay cheque that would change their life, and everyone goes home happy.'

Victoria sat back, a smile wide across her face.

Yes, it sounded completely insane, offering herself up to some stranger, but it was exactly the sort of plan Daddy would have come up with. And while she was sure it wasn't what he'd planned on when he wrote that bloody awful clause in his will, she knew he'd be proud of her for finding a solution to get what she wanted.

She watched the idea take seed inside her assistant's head. Trying to work out the ins and outs of how to go about finding such a person; after all, one couldn't just put a personal ad out there. Victoria wasn't even sure they did personal ads anymore. They had probably moved to social media. One simply took a selfie and popped it on Instagram with the words, *Husband wanted! Willing to pay handsomely for a handsome husband. Please attach your curriculum vitae to your photograph as a reply. #MarryMe #Timelimit #Before35!*

'Okay,' her secretary said slowly, shifting in her chair to sit forward and lean on the desk as if she was sure her employer had gone mad and didn't want to spook her. 'Say we did that, find someone willing to marry you for a… fee, it's not going to be a simple or quick task.'

Victoria was about to push the file across the desk to show her she already had someone in mind when Kirstie continued.

'If you were merely an heiress to your father's fortune, things might be different, but you're a member of the *Royal Family*. This person won't just be scrutinised by business associates, but by the King himself, by your family, the media, and by the *world*. If I had the time to prep this hypothetical man, the idea might have some merit, but not only do we have a time restraint, there's another *minor* problem…'

Victoria frowned. What hadn't she thought of?

'You have to have a baby with him.'

Oh. Yes, the baby clause.

'And *naturally*,' Kirstie prompted her, her face screaming *think about this!* 'You're going to have to sleep with this person again and again… and *again* until you get pregnant. And I hate to be unkind, but at your age we all know it can take longer to happen. There's so much evidence of women in their thirties having less chance of getting pregnant. So, you're going to have to sleep with this stranger that you're *paying*, every night.'

Her fingers danced over the edge of the file, itching to find the picture of Cormac with just a towel around his waist, glistening with water after a shower at the gym. The idea of him in her bed every night really wasn't going to be a hardship, she decided.

'And even if you could find yourself doing such a thing, what's going to happen when you *have* a baby? Will it be over and done with once the baby is here or do you keep the marriage going for the whole five years? When you do go your separate ways, will he get access to the child? Would he even *want* access? Would you want him to have access? But the child would be his too and he'd be legally entitled to it—unless you write it into the contract that he couldn't see the child.

'But would you even want anyone who would consider or accept *that* as part of a contract in the first place? I mean what type of man would he be if he's willing to walk away from a child he helped to create? And what if you *can't* get pregnant? Does that break the deal? How would you pay him? Would he spill everything to the-'

'Okay, you've made your point.' Victoria slumped back into her seat, feeling defeated. Everything Kirstie said were points she hadn't considered. She was so stupid. Especially for thinking she could ever compare herself to her father, with his sharp mind and business acumen.

'Victoria, my lady, I'm sorry but this is what you pay me for-'

'You mean *did* pay you for,' Victoria muttered, folding her arms across her chest in a childish pout. She stared down at the table and winced as she heard Kirstie growl in frustration.

'We've been over this. You'll back pay me as soon as

you're married.' Victoria heard the rustling of pages as Kirstie moved things around, rearranging herself so she could begin to organise herself again. Victoria knew she was already trying to formulate a new idea to help her.

Victoria glanced upwards as Kirstie reached for the file on Cormac Blake. 'What's this?'

'Nothing,' Victoria snapped. She grabbed the file from under Kirstie's fingers and threw it back into the drawer, slamming it shut. She glanced out of the window again, unwilling to meet her assistant's surprised face. 'You're dismissed,' she grumbled.

She listened to her personal secretary gather her things and quietly slip out of the room, closing the door behind her with a soft click, giving Victoria the space she needed to seethe.

She toed at the carpet with her foot as she mulled over the points Kirstie had raised. *If* she went to Cormac with the proposition and *if* he accepted, they would have to sleep together… Victoria couldn't help the smile that touched her lips as she recalled Cormac's well-defined chest, how hard it had felt against her body and how it had glistened under the dim lights. She'd never admit to it out loud, but there had been a couple of nights where she'd dreamt of running her hands over that chest, having her body pressed against it again—this time naked—as it arched up to meet hers.

She cleared her throat, shaking her head to dismiss the wispy memories of dreams from her mind. She glanced at the desk drawer from the corner of her eye and worried her lower lip with her teeth.

Sleeping with Cormac Blake really wouldn't be a hardship, but the other questions remained. She had no doubt he'd be willing to father a child. The dossier said he was raising his brother as if he was Cormac's own son, and if the school reports on James Blake were accurate, he was doing a very good job, so he probably *would* want to be involved in raising any child they conceived. Victoria mulled on that detail for a moment and decided that she was more than fine with the idea. In fact, it only made her feel more certain that she'd made the right decision in picking Cormac for the job.

She bit her lip as she slowly reached down for the folder in her drawer. Perhaps another read-through—and a glance at *that* picture again—would make things a little clearer.

After all, it wouldn't hurt to be completely certain one way or the other…

CHAPTER SEVEN

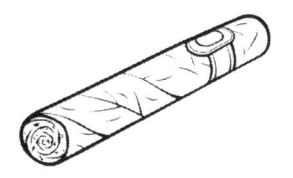

The thrum of the beat vibrated through the floor of the stage as Cormac turned and twisted in time with the music, following his fellow dancers as the choreographer put them through their paces. Cormac hated the start of the new season; new dances to learn, new teams to work with, and the start of the summer wedding season would mean plenty of handsy hen parties to contend with.

'Cormac! It's spin, down, *then* bring your head up as your bounce that behind!'

'Sorry, Magda!' he shouted to the exasperated dance expert.

'A week,' the woman shouted. 'These dances go live in a week and you're all a shamble!'

'Her hair is a shamble,' Harry whispered next to him as they ambled to the side of the stage to grab a quick drink of water.

'Be nice,' Cormac chided, before hiding his grin behind his own bottle as he took a deep gulp of the chilled drink. 'You know her boyfriend left her last week.'

'Heard he left her for a younger model, and I do *not* blame him,' the other man said, as he wiped his brow with a fluffy white towel. 'I'm the last man to find women sexually attractive, but even I know when a dog's barking.'

Cormac's drink sprayed across the stage at Harry's words, causing the rest of the dance team to turn and look their way.

'Stop being a bitch, Harry,' Cormac said between coughing fits as his friend laughed at his side. 'It doesn't become you.'

'Darling, *anything* becomes me,' Harry said in a faux feminine voice as he fluttered his lashes at the other man.

Cormac was about to reply when Geri's hurried call from backstage distracted him.

'What's up, my blue wonder?' he asked as he grabbed his own towel and wrapped it around his neck before heading in her direction. 'You gotta stop coming down and perving on us,' he said, throwing her a wink. 'People are going to start to think you're obsessed with naked men- Whoa, hey!' Cormac almost fell over as Geri grabbed his arm and forcefully pulled him into the shadowed wings of the stage.

'Shut up and listen,' she hissed, poking her head around the curtain to try and see out into the front of the club. 'I just overheard Britney,' she added hurriedly. 'Apparently, we're about to get a very special visitor.'

Cormac instantly thought back to last week, to Lady Victoria staring up at him as she disappeared down the stairs. Was the royal coming back? Did she want to see the club where she'd been rescued? Try and work out what had happened that night? Perhaps, it was the Guard or the police asking her to do a walk-through to try and jog her memory —they did that sort of stuff for crimes all the time, didn't they?

Or maybe, just maybe, Cormac dared to fantasise a little, perhaps she just wanted to come and thank him and see him one more time.

Surely, the moment he'd experienced couldn't have been one-sided. Could it?

He shook his head of the daft thoughts. The woman was royalty, an heiress, and ten years older than he was; women like her didn't look at guys like him except for a quick weekend of fun. He'd been there and done that before, and certainly wasn't looking for a repeat of it, no matter how caught up by her he'd been.

'Ow!' Cormac cried, snatching his arm from Geri's clutches. 'Did you just *pinch* me?'

'Are you even *listening* to me?' she demanded with a huff. Heat filled Cormac's cheeks, tinging them pink. 'You're adorable, Cormac, and still very green here, so you need to shut up and listen to me. Conner O'Malley is supposed to be coming down here today.'

Cormac frowned. He didn't recognise the name.

'Oh, c'mon!' Geri groaned. 'You *have* to know who that is? How the hell do you not know *anything*?'

'Well sorry if I'm not able to read the gossip columns on whatever website talks about the rich and famous or watch mindless television night after night. But in case you haven't noticed I've been raising a kid on my own for the last six years after losing *both* my parents.' He glared at his friend before beginning to march away, but Geri grabbed hold of his arm again and tried to pull him to a stop.

'I'm sorry, I know, and I shouldn't have said that, but you need to *listen* to me.'

The panic in her voice gave Cormac pause, and he stopped his attempt to get rid of the little minx and stared down at her.

'Spill, Smurfette.'

'You know she had blue *skin*, right?' the woman sighed, rolling her eyes at him. 'Whatever, Conner O'Malley is the owner of Fortune Holdings, the parent company of Star Entertainment, which, through various other channels, owns

Pleasure Heights Inc.' She gave him a look that said, *think this through*. Cormac furrowed his brow. That did sound familiar. 'For God's sake, Cormac, I know you're pretty, but I thought you were smart! That's who owns the club! And about fifty others across the country! This is the big boss of the big boss of several more big bosses of our boss! He's the great-great-great granddaddy of all bosses!'

'And why do you need to drag me off stage for that? If he's coming down to check us out, then surely you'd want me out there practising.'

Geri shook her head again. 'I overheard Britney say *your* name *and* Lady Snape's name. Cormac, I think he's coming to see *you*!'

Cormac took a deep breath, holding it so it puffed out his cheeks as he slowly released it. Well, shit. This could go several ways. The worst being that he'd be fired for consequently letting the Guard on the premises—no one wanted that for their company's reputation—or he was being rewarded for a member of the Royal Family being snapped sneaking out of the back of the club. That could put *Monty's* on the map with some better clientele, and they'd all love that. Bigger spenders would equal more money coming into the club, meaning pay rises and bigger tips for the dancers.

He prayed it was the latter reason, but with the way his luck had been running these past eighteen months, hanging onto everything by the skin of his teeth, he'd bet his last bit that it'd be closer to the former.

'I want to take it from the top! Where are my dancers!' Magda's voice called out, and the pounding of feet scrambling into place rumbled across the stage.

'Sorry, I gotta go,' Cormac said, pushing his bottle of water into Geri's hands and dashing towards his place. 'Keep me posted!' he called as he flung the towel towards her. Geri grabbed it but dropped the bottle in the process.

He laughed at Geri's lack of grace as she chased the

rolling bottle, trying to stop it from going onto the stage and into the dancers' way when a commotion at the front of the house caught everyone's attention.

'What in God's name is it now?' Magda's shrill, frustrated voice echoed throughout the theatre as she turned to look. She pressed a button on a remote she was holding which brought up the lights in the club so they could see who was coming in unannounced.

A wave of whispers started as their eyes fell on the group that waltzed through the door as if they owned the place. At six-foot-three inches, Cormac was considered tall by Avalonian standards, but the two men at the front of the group were taller than him—by at least half a foot!—and almost as wide.

'Wouldn't want to meet them in a dark alley,' Harry muttered to Cormac's left. 'Or maybe I would!' The man laughed quietly, but Cormac couldn't find the amusement in it. He swallowed as two more men, not quite as tall but just as wide, followed not far behind the first pair; if Conner O'Malley needed such men for protection, just how big a deal was the man?

The front two men stepped aside and a small, rotund man with receding dark hair stepped forward, a fat cigar clenched between his lips as he took in the club. The man nodded his head as he walked slowly around the floor, running his finger along the edges of the tables, picking out the roses from the little plastic vases in the middle of them before moving forward towards the stage again.

The dancers on the stage shifted uncomfortably.

They were all big men, muscular and toned, but they weren't fighters. Cormac had been a mixed martial arts junior champion in his teenage years, which was how he'd toned his body so well, but he'd never been in a fight outside the ring. And certainly not for the last few years. He also knew if one of those four bodyguards had stepped into the ring during a competition, he'd probably have thrown in the towel right away.

'And just *who* are you?' Magda asked haughtily. 'And smoking indoors in a public place is *illegal*.'

The short man puffed on his cigar some more as he played with a tablecloth between his fingers. 'I'm none of your concern,' he said, dropping the covering back to the table. He held the woman's gaze and tapped the ash from the thick, brown toro onto the crisp white linen. 'But who you lot are, or at least one of you, concerns *me*.'

Cormac swallowed, watching the man narrow his eyes as he took in each of their faces. He had to act surprised, which he was sure wasn't going to be a problem.

'I'm looking for our little hero from last week, I understand-'

O'Malley didn't need to finish his sentence, as every head in the club turned to stare at Cormac at the word *hero*.

'That'd be me, then,' Cormac said wearily, lifting his hand to give his so-called ultimate boss a single wave. O'Malley popped his cigar back in his mouth and smiled around the thick stogie as his eyes drank Cormac in.

'Oh, you'll do nicely,' the man said, waving Cormac to him.

He climbed off the stage and followed the smaller man as he walked towards the back of the club where the VIP tables were set up. O'Malley fell into one of the chairs, his legs barely touching the floor when he wiggled back into the deep cushions to get comfortable. The man began playing with his phone as he puffed on the sickening cigar.

'Sit,' O'Malley said with a wave of one hand to the chair opposite. Cormac did as he was bid, biting his lip so as not to ask questions. Finally, the man put away his phone and pulled the stogie from his mouth. 'So, lad, heard you played Prince Charming to one of our Royal Family the other night.'

'Well, I wouldn't say that, exactly-'

'No, no, don't you put yourself down,' O'Malley interrupted, pointing his yellowing fingers that held his cigar at Cormac. 'You did well…?'

'Cormac. Cormac Blake, sir.'

'Cormac.' O'Malley leaned back and stared at him, his brow creasing in thought. Cormac resisted the temptation to shift in his seat; for all the women—and men—he'd had stare at him as he stripped out of his clothes, he'd never felt more naked than he did at that moment.

'Yeah, you'll do nicely.' O'Malley didn't comment further as he stuck the cigar back into his mouth and puffed. 'Tell me what happened then.'

'Er, well,' he began, telling the older man everything he'd seen and what had happened once he'd taken Lady Victoria inside. He didn't mention how he'd felt attracted to the Lady of the Realm or their moment as she descended the stairs. O'Malley found it amusing that she'd managed to overcome him, and *extremely* interested when he mentioned her and the Head of the Royal Guard, probing for more information. Cormac kept it to the facts and kept how he'd thought at times they'd seemed *awfully familiar* with one another to himself.

'And then they left.' He finished his tale with a shrug. 'I went to see Axel about getting any security footage we might have. As far as I know, he gave it to one of the police officers before they disappeared.'

'And you didn't go to the press about this?'

'Absolutely not, sir!'

O'Malley raised one eyebrow as he peered at him through the smoke that surrounded his head. 'You didn't even think about it, did you, boy?' It wasn't really a question, but Cormac shook his head anyway. 'A *real* Prince Charming after all.'

O'Malley looked towards one of his men and gave him a firm nod. The man turned, twisted his finger in the air, and the other three men did the same before stepping away from the VIP booth. Cormac watched them as they formed a line between the rest of the club and the VIP section, all with their backs to their boss.

'Um,' he began, but O'Malley cut him off again.

'How'd you like to earn a little more than you're getting now?'

Cormac made to speak, but then promptly closed his mouth again. Such an offer didn't come without a catch.

'Good lad, you learn fast.' The man took a final puff on his cigar before putting it out on the table between them. Cormac frowned down at the mashed-up toro sticking up out of its ashes. 'I understand you have a few debts.'

That caught Cormac's attention. He was waiting for an eviction notice any day now and he'd been desperately trying to find a way to earn a few extra crowns quickly.

'Now you're listening,' O'Malley sighed, sitting back. 'It's my understanding that someone is doing some background checks on you-'

'On me? Why?' he asked, sitting up straighter.

The man looked at him like he was stupid. 'You rescued a member of the Royal Family and you're wondering *why* someone is checking on you.'

Well, when he put it that way, that made sense.

'My source tells me that pretty soon, you're going to receive an invitation to meet her Ladyship, and I want you to do just that.'

'Well, if she asks, of course I'd go. But I don't understand how this gets me more money.'

'All you have to do'—the man paused to consider his words carefully—'is tell me exactly what Lady Victoria offers you. You do that and I'll clear all your debts *and* give you a nice little raise.'

'A raise?' Cormac's eyes grew wide at that.

'How about double what you get now, and I'll even give

you fifty percent on top of your tips if… Well, I'll decide what earns you that when you tell me what she offers.'

'And that's all I have to do? Tell you what she offers me? What if she doesn't offer me anything? What if she meets me just to say thanks?'

'If that's all there is to it, that's all there is to it. I'll still clear your debts and give you the pay rise. A deal's a deal, after all.' O'Malley shrugged as if it was of no consequence to him, but the fact he wanted this in the first place told Cormac that whatever it was his boss *thought* he was going to be offered was probably worth a lot more.

But it bothered him that the man even wanted this information in the first place. It seemed a bit much that the *granddaddy of all bosses* would come all the way down here to meet him and offer him everything he had just to get a little bit of gossip. Was he hoping he could find out something big enough to sell to the world media for a good price? Or maybe he wanted to blackmail her…

'I'm feeling that you don't like Lady Victoria; why?'

A slow, wide grin spread across O'Malley's face. 'You're good, lad. Let's just say,' he said as he pushed himself forward to stand up. 'That her father was a pain in my arse the whole time he was alive. Every deal we went head-to-head for, he always won.'

Cormac frowned. 'But that's got nothing to do with Lady Victoria.'

'How do you think he did it? Who do you think had access to contacts he and I didn't?'

The cogs in Cormac's brain turned as he considered Victoria's position in the Royal Family. She went to exclusive events hosted by some of the world's most rich and famous, met kings and queens, and talked with prime ministers and presidents from all over the world. There was certainly something to take away from each event and even if people like Conner O'Malley could get into them, Patrick Snape had the advantage that his daughter could access places at such occasions that others couldn't.

'That's not... ethical,' Cormac said quietly, rather disappointed that the innocent damsel he'd rescued wasn't exactly lily white.

'Atta boy.' O'Malley sounded almost proud at him for coming to the right conclusion. The man finally stood up. 'She's been a damn pain in my arse for over fifteen years. So, you in?'

She'd done the same to the man in front of him, Cormac reasoned. Telling her father things only she'd gained access to, and all *he* had to do was tell the man what she offered, nothing more. If she offered nothing, it still meant he kept a roof over his head. He couldn't see any bad coming from this.

But that was how he'd got himself into his current situation in the first place. He hadn't seen what could go wrong, hadn't seen all the risks involved with taking a gamble.

He couldn't see what harm there was in telling someone you got a fancy meal and a thank you or given a simple token of appreciation. Maybe showing off a gift of diamond cufflinks or something equally stupid; people like her probably didn't even realise that regular Joes like him wore shirts with *buttons* at the cuffs if they wore shirts at all. Cormac wasn't even sure he owned a smart shirt anymore—at least not one he didn't rip off night after night.

Cormac sat back, looking at the short man. He licked his lips as his mind whirled. It was an amazing offer, but every single bet he'd placed in his life had fallen short.

'I'm sorry, Mr O'Malley,' Cormac said as he slowly stood up. He towered over his boss, but he was the one who felt threatened as the other man narrowed his gaze at Cormac. 'I don't feel comfortable with that kind of arrangement.'

'Are you stupid or something, kid?'

Cormac wanted to huff a laugh. He'd flown through school, was in the top ten percent of his year group when he graduated with a first-class Secondary Education Diploma, he read textbooks in his spare time, and tried to teach James concepts when he came home complaining he was stuck on certain topics in school. Yet all that academic greatness hadn't helped in these kinds of situations.

'No, sir,' he decided to say instead. 'I just don't feel comfortable revealing that kind of thing.'

'Interesting, considering your line of work.' Cormac's mouth dropped at the snide remark. 'Well, there's always option B.'

Cormac raised his brow. 'And that would be?'

'That I fire your arse.'

∼

CORMAC PUT THE KEY IN THE LOCK AND STOPPED. HE DROPPED his head to the door and leaned his weight against it, resisting the urge to bang it against the flimsy wood to see if that would knock some sense into him. He took a deep breath, puffing up his cheeks as he slowly released it while trying to gather his thoughts.

How was he going to tell his brother he'd been sacked? How could he explain to a six-year-old that they were about to lose their tiny, shitty home because Cormac had *morals*— which was ironic considering he took his clothes off for money. James would tell him he could get another job as a waiter; they'd be fine in his simple child-like view of the world. He had no idea that waiting tables was not the part of his job that brought in the money.

'Fuck!' Cormac breathed the word as he recalled the bills sitting on the table. He remembered the rent arrears piling up week in, week out. He thought of how his bank balance hadn't seen the colour black in over a year…

Maybe he could go back and tell O'Malley he'd do it? He'd

tell him everything if Lady Victoria came to see him… And he'd hate himself forever.

But what was a little self-hatred piled on top of self-pity, isolation, near celibacy, and…

'Yeah, that's enough, Cormac,' he said to himself as he stood up straight again. He squared his shoulders, gave himself a mental slap, and turned the key. He'd understood what he was letting himself in for when he'd sat down years ago with the social workers and defended his right to be James' guardian. They'd warned him of these things, told him it would be difficult, that he was young and had no idea what he was letting himself in for… It was the only risk he'd taken that he hadn't regretted.

Until tonight.

He'd been holding on by the skin of his teeth to provide for James; maybe he had to face that he *couldn't* do this anymore and perhaps James would be better off without him.

The idea of James in a loving home with a mother and father doting on him, making him healthy home-cooked meals that were heaped high on his plate, driving him to school in a car that was actually safe for him, dressing him in clothes they bought new from actual clothes shops and not the charity stores he had to visit without James just so the kid wouldn't know his clothes were second-hand… The thought both turned his stomach at the idea of not being there to do all that *and* filled him with longing that James could have it all if he was just willing to let go.

He swallowed down the guilt that he'd done James a disservice in trying to raise him, from not putting him up for adoption when he was still a baby like his social worker had advised. He turned the key in the lock. A scramble from the living room caught his attention and his stomach dropped a little at the idea he'd scared Mrs Battersea with his early return.

God, he was going to have to fire her too.

'You're early,' she said with a sigh of relief as she came to the doorway of the sitting room. 'Is everything— Oh no.' He watched her shoulders drop as she realised the situation immediately. It must have been written on his face; he'd never been particularly good at hiding his feelings.

'I'm sorry,' he whispered, his voice cracking a little.

'Me too,' she said softly, stepping towards him. 'You guys have gone through enough as is. You two need a break, not more crap piled on top.'

Cormac couldn't answer her; his throat suddenly seemed blocked and his vision went blurry as her selfless words touched his heart.

'Oh, lad,' she said, her small, chubby frame waddling to him. 'It's okay to cry and let it go sometimes.' She wrapped her arms around his waist and pulled him in for a hug. Her head barely reached his chest, but Cormac leaned into her, throwing his arms around her, and bowing his head as low as it would go as the tears came.

He would cry right now, and then he'd be able to face James tomorrow.

'Cup of tea, I think,' Mrs Battersea said, untangling herself when his quiet sobs turned to sniffles. She grabbed his hand and led him to his small kitchen, seating him at the table and proceeding to potter around within its tiny confines.

'Why don't you tell me what happened?' Cormac shook his head, but found the words pouring from his mouth of their own accord. He started with how he'd found Lady Victoria, O'Malley trying to blackmail him, and subsequently firing him for not agreeing to break the confidence of his princess.

'But why didn't you agree?' the woman asked as she took the seat opposite, her own cup in hand. 'I mean, it's not as if you owe The Lady Snape anything; you already saved her backside once.'

He took a deep drink of the tea she made far too milky, appreciating the fact that it might help him fall asleep later.

'You didn't see her that night,' Cormac began to explain. 'She kept mentioning her grandfather finding out, the media attention… Her life isn't her own. And from what O'Malley said, I'm not sure if her father didn't control her somewhat too.' The woman nodded her grey-haired head along as if she'd always thought the same. 'Say she comes and meets me and gives me something nice, and I tell him, and it gets out—with the whole back story—I'm no better than anyone else in her life.'

As he spoke, some of the guilt that had opened a chasm deep in his stomach eased, but Mrs Battersea *tsked* as she shook her head and put down her cup, staring him in the eye.

'Young man, unless that woman gives you a few thousand crowns for what you did, you should've taken the offer that boss of yours gave.' Her voice was firm and brooked no room for argument. 'Don't think I don't see the bills on the side, the final demand letters, *or* the bank statements lined in red. She's a rich lady with lots of connections; a few stories here and there in the paper is the *least* she can expect for her life of luxury and comfort. She can look after herself. You've got to look after you and that brother of yours.'

'Mrs Battersea, please,' he began, shifting in his seat as the pit of dread and unease opened in his stomach again.

'Oh no, don't you go defending her again. She already had you do that once, you're not her personal knight in shining armour!' She snatched the empty cup from his hand and stood up. 'Girls like her, they expect everyone to run around and do exactly as they say. Snap their fingers and obey their every whim. They step on people like you and me every damn day.' She ran the cups under the tap, squeezing far too much washing-up liquid into them. 'Little people like us are full of their footprints; we're left living down in places like this, scrambling around for a scrap of something they leave over.'

Cormac hung his head, his heart pounding in his chest as he realised the mistake he'd made. She was right. How many people had screwed him over? Used his youth to scam him? They had run off without looking back, without a notch of guilt in their hearts. They were living on his money and every other poor sap's savings they'd managed to con while he struggled to feed his small family and keep a roof over their heads.

'You go back down to that place tomorrow and you ask to meet that boss of yours. Tell him you changed your mind-'

'I don't think-'

'And that's your problem,' she said, slapping down the dish-brush and turning around to face him. 'You don't think!' Cormac's eyes widened at the woman's fury, completely caught off guard by the venom he could feel pouring from her every pore. What the hell had happened to the old woman to feel such hatred towards people she didn't know?

She sighed as she stared at his flabbergasted face.

'I'm sorry, Cormac. You're a good kid with a big heart. And for it to still be so good after what the world has thrown at you… It just makes me want to scream and rage at the injustice in the world.'

He managed a weak smile and nodded quickly.

'Think about what I said,' she told him as she pressed a kiss to the top of his head. 'I won't say anything more, or to anyone else-'

'Thank you.'

'-but you take a long hard think about what I just said.'

'I will.' She patted his cheek before leaving the kitchen. He watched from his chair as she collected her coat from where it hung on the living room door and shrugged herself into it. 'You need me to walk you home?' he asked. She only lived three doors away, but he offered every night he came home, and every night she gave the same answer.

'I think I can manage.'

The door closed quietly behind her, and Cormac stared at the space she'd left.

The minutes slipped by as he gazed blankly into the hallway from his seat. The old clock ticked on the wall above the sink, counting the seconds, but Cormac didn't hear it, didn't even notice the dripping from the tap that always happened when he didn't turn the thing tight enough. It drove him mad when he was trying to sleep, always forcing him out of his blanket cocoon, but now it didn't even register.

No other clubs would touch him once O'Malley got the word out to them, he'd been told until he had a better car, he couldn't taxi, and waiting tables just didn't provide anywhere near what he needed.

He was going to lose everything.

He was going to lose James.

He licked his lips, feeling the dry and cracked skin there, telling him he'd been staring into space far longer than he'd thought. He swallowed as he stood up, his eyes still on the front door.

James would be fine for a few minutes, he reasoned as he stepped through it and closed it behind him. He walked down to the bottom of the stairs, almost as if he was in a trance, being called to the payphone that miraculously still worked in this cesspit of an estate.

He pulled the number he'd been slipped before he'd left the club earlier and dropped the only slivers he had on him into the phone. He carefully dialled each digit, his heart picking up speed with each button he pressed.

The line clicked and it began to ring.

And ring.

He closed his eyes but couldn't decide if he wanted to

pray for the line to be answered or for it to be ignored. He felt his breathing quickening with each trill down the line and his stomach twisted into a nervous knot.

The ringing suddenly stopped.

Cormac gulped, suddenly unsure what to say or even if he could speak at all.

'Glad you came to your senses, lad.' Cormac closed his eyes, his stomach sinking deep inside. 'But the deal's changed.'

'What?' he breathed.

'You had your chance.'

'But I-'

'Don't worry, lad.' It sounded like the man took a puff on his cigar. Cormac's mind absently wondered how many of the things he smoked a day. 'I'll still see you okay—*if* the stuff you give me is good enough.' Cormac shut his eyes, cursing himself.

'*But*, seeing as you rescued a member of royalty and got us some *very* positive press, I'll drop what you need in your account to clear off the arrears on that shit hole you call a home.'

Cormac's heart leapt. He wouldn't get evicted. He wouldn't be homeless. He wouldn't have to lose his brother.

'Thank you, sir,' he said in relief.

'Don't mention it, kid.' The man paused. 'And I *mean* that.' Cormac nodded before remembering the other man couldn't see him.

'Yes, sir.'

'Now when she meets with you, you call me back on this number, you understand?'

'Yes, sir.'

Another puff on the cigar. 'I like you, lad. Don't let me down.'

The line went dead and the sound of coins dropping into the cash box below the phone echoed through the empty car park. Cormac stared at the receiver before slowly putting it back in its cradle.

He felt like he'd just made a deal with the Devil, but if there were such a thing, he was being a lot more generous than God had ever been to him.

Cormac shoved his hands deep into his pocket, trying to shake off the feeling he'd just stepped into something he really shouldn't have as he slowly walked back to the flat. He only had to meet the princess and tell his boss what she'd said. It was only what she'd done for her father, he reminded himself again.

And again.

And again.

The walk back home had never seemed so long.

CHAPTER EIGHT

*V*ictoria's well-manicured fingers played with the manila file at her side as the Rolls Royce slipped easily through the Avon streets. The dazzling lights of the bay fell away as they moved into parts of the city she'd never been to before. She frowned, watching the landscape changing from bright white skyscrapers or towers made of glass, to concrete blocks of grey and brown that grew shorter and more decrepit the farther they travelled.

'This is the address, ma'am,' her driver announced, pulling into a courtyard surrounded by buildings she could only describe as derelict. Clothing hung across tatty balconies, paint peeled from doors and window frames, and rubbish littered the streets as it spilt from giant bins half-pushed into alcoves under the block of flats. Cars that looked rusted and unsalvageable were discarded across the pavements around the yard, as if the drivers had parked and then simply given up on them.

Victoria stared in shock as children, covered in dust and mud, ran wild between the disused vehicles as others used the cars as climbing frames, screaming and shouting as they went. One claimed to be the king of the yard as he climbed atop an old 4x4 and dared the others to try and overthrow him.

'Are you sure we're at the right address?' Victoria asked, unable to take her eyes from the children who scaled the vehicle to try and dethrone their king. What if one of them fell and cut themselves? They'd get tetanus or some other nasty infection. Where on earth were their parents?

One of the children scrambled up on the car's bonnet and shouted *charge!* and Victoria did a double-take as she reached for the file next to her. She quickly rifled through it while the children continued to scream and shout as they clambered up the dilapidated car, and pulled a set of photos from within its pages. She glanced down at one of the photographs, taken only days ago, of the same young boy dressed smartly in a school uniform jumping into the waiting arms of Cormac Blake.

James Ross Blake, the younger brother and only living relative of Cormac Dean Blake, was the daring leader of the resistance. This was definitely the right place.

Victoria took a deep breath before silently nodding to the driver. She waited for him to open the door, reminding herself that this was the right thing to do over and over in her mind as the cries of the feral bunch outside raged on.

When the door opened and she climbed out of the back of the elegant car, she couldn't help the wrinkle of her nose at the smell that assaulted her. She quickly smoothed her face back into the one of polite interest she relied on during all royal events as she glanced towards the overflowing bins and swallowed down the bile threatening to rise in her throat.

'*Oooh,*' came a girlish voice from Victoria's left. 'Pretty!' Victoria turned to see a small, dust-covered child, whose hair she assumed had been blonde before someone had dunked her in a mud bath, grinning up at her with a semi-toothless smile. She couldn't have been older than four, perhaps five years old at the most.

Victoria marvelled; at the girl's age, she'd already learnt the finer points of dining room etiquette, the correct addresses for each noble line and world dignitary, and was beginning to be taught points of needlework and other arts and crafts fit for a lady of her standing. Mud baths and imaginary conquests on fictitious kings had never factored into her upbringing—although there'd been a number of occasions since those days when she'd imagined her grandfather being overthrown.

'Are you a princess?' the girl asked, the end of the word *princess* whistling between her missing front teeth. Victoria offered the girl a small smile, crouching down to be eye level with her.

'No, I'm not,' she told the little one honestly. The girl's face fell with disappointment and Victoria dropped her voice to whisper conspiratorially, 'But I do know a couple—they lent me their car.'

The girl's blue eyes went wide as she turned them on the long Rolls Royce and Victoria stood back up to take her leave. 'Shiny,' the young child said.

'Don't let the boys climb on it,' Victoria added with a wink as she headed towards the staircase with the numbers 20-39 written on a sign next to it. Cormac and his brother lived in number 35, so she assumed he'd be towards the top.

She wasn't wrong. Six flights of stairs later and she was on the third-floor landing labelled 34-39, and deeply regretting her choice of footwear.

She smoothed out the wrinkles in her summer dress and pulled her compact from her bag. She checked her smile and ran her fingers through her hair, before holding her head high and squaring her shoulders as she shoved the mirror back in her bag. She took another deep breath and headed to the address on the file under her arm.

Number 35 was one of the flats with a door adorned not only with peeling paint, but with the added aesthetic of silver tape patching up a crack in the glass that ran diagonally from one corner of the thin pane to the other. She hesitated to knock; her hand posed ready to tap on the wood. What would she find inside? Was Cormac Blake the kind of man who willingly lived in such a state? Was this perfectly acceptable to him?

She glanced at the file as she nibbled at the corner of her lower lip. The file hadn't said anything within its pages about Cormac being such a man, but it hadn't said he wasn't either.

Perhaps she should have given Marcus longer, allowed the guard to conduct proper surveillance as he'd requested, get the real nitty-gritty on her Prince Charming.

She licked her lips as she considered turning around and dashing back to the waiting car, but at the last minute she drew herself back up, shaking her head. No, she could and *would* do this, she decided, letting out a small growl of determination as she sharply rapped on the door with her knuckle.

She waited a moment. Then a beat longer, before knocking again just as a shadow appeared in the window and a muffled voice said something that sounded vaguely like an irritated, *I'm coming*. She cursed herself for her impatience.

'Yo,' Cormac said as he swung the door open. His mouth froze around the O sound as he saw who was standing on the other side of the door.

Victoria stared back. Her hazy memories from the previous week recalled him being handsome, and she definitely remembered being attracted to her hero. The photographs Marcus had acquired for her not only reinforced her memories but gave her something solid on which to judge him. A definite nine to her… what had her cousin Artie rated her? A five. A six at a push, but only when she allowed someone else to help her get ready. The bastard.

But Cormac in the flesh… Well, jeans and a t-shirt, she lamented, vaguely recalling smooth, tanned skin, well-defined muscles, and a stomach she wanted to trace with her tongue.

She shook herself of her thoughts. Dressed or not, the man was a *ten*. The demi-god she kept dreaming about wasn't a memory exaggerated by the drugs Simon had sneaked into her system. No, the man was bona-fide Hollywood-level handsome and then some.

'Mr Blake,' Victoria said and thanked her stars her voice sounded normal. 'I don't know if you remember me, but I'm-'

'Lady Victoria Snape,' he finished for her. 'I couldn't forget you.'

'That's… good…' Victoria replied, unsure of what to say after being interrupted. 'I've… come to pay my thanks,' she said, her smile straining slightly as she glanced over his shoulder into his abode, hoping he'd get the hint. Standing on a doorstep for all the world to see was not exactly what she'd planned for this meeting, and by now it would have been polite to have invited her inside.

'Aw, you didn't have to do that,' he said as he leaned against the door frame, bobbing his head slightly as his cheeks turned pink. The colour made his dusting of freckles stand out, and Victoria had to resist the urge to reach out and trace them, connecting them up to see what pattern they'd make.

'I'd have done it for anyone in need. Just wish I'd got to get my hands on that prick- I mean… er…' He glanced up at her looking at little lost and giving Victoria a chance to refocus on what they were talking about.

'Prick is more than apt, I think,' she reassured him with a genuine smile. It was a far tamer word than any of the ones her sisters had used for the pathetic excuse of a man. Hattie had even created a few new ones.

Finally, she sighed and simply asked, 'Mr Blake, may I come inside?'

The man straightened up, and Victoria couldn't help a quick glance at the bulge of his arm as it flexed with the movement.

'Of- of course,' he said, his voice thick with mortification at his own lack of manners. He stepped back to allow her entry to the tiny hallway and motioned to a room off to the right before closing the door behind them.

Victoria entered a tiny reception room, taking in the heady scent of *man* and all that it meant. This wasn't just a reception room, she realised as she glanced around, taking in a small two-seater couch, a bookcase, an extremely *old* television set, and a small table a stack of papers sat upon. This doubled as a bedroom. It had that distinct scent of *man* she remembered from Marcus' own room whenever she'd sneaked into his barracks.

She wondered what it would be like to be wrapped up in such a scent again, to feel the touch of a man who desired her, wanted her, begged her to let him have his way with her-

'Would you like something to drink?' Victoria jumped at Cormac's unsure voice from near the doorway. She glanced at him over her shoulder, feeling the heat scorching her cheeks, and hoped he didn't notice. The way his eyes roamed over her form, lingering on her small, pert behind made her pulse quicken as she wondered if he'd had similar thoughts of her. Maybe he'd like to saunter over to her, press his firm, hot body against hers. Nestle his thick, hard-

'Some tea?' he asked, his voice a little lower than before. 'A glass of water?'

'Tea would be lovely, thank you.'

He nodded and turned, heading through the adjacent door she assumed led to the kitchen.

She took a deep breath to focus back on her task and took another quick take of the room. Her eyes once more landed

on the papers on the small table and out of habit, she gave them a brief glance, not enough for anyone to think anything more than her taking in her surroundings out of politeness, but enough for her to see what was on the topmost paper—a trick she'd picked up working for her father. She noted the thick red header on most of the letters she spied on the haphazard pile, but it was the words *Eviction Notice* that really drew her eye. Carefully, she used a single finger to lift the stack of papers and count how many final demands she could see.

Four, including the eviction letter. Marcus' report had said he needed financial help, but it hadn't detailed in what way. She'd figured he was living on the poverty line, not beyond it. There had been no indications of gambling debts or drug addictions, and she knew *those* would have been instant flags on Marcus' radar. So, was this merely normal for people of Cormac's standing? Did everyone in this area receive such bills?

Victoria frowned. She'd never received a bill. Everything was always handled by her father's accountants. Her credit cards, hotel rooms, her private staff… not once did she see the expense her lifestyle cost.

She dropped the letters, annoyed at herself for being so oblivious to life around her, and moved around the room. She took in the few pictures he had on the walls and on the one bookcase the room held; the volumes were not fiction, but titles of politics, mathematics, and law. She frowned at them for a moment before glancing at the pictures again, noting they were all of family. No friends, no landscapes, just Cormac, James, and a couple she assumed were their parents.

The frames were tatty, some partly broken and held together by tape more than anything else, but they were still proudly shown. A wedding picture of the couple she supposed were his parents hung in the middle of a wall of other various pictures of them throughout their lives. Some had Cormac with them, while some were simply of the man or the woman. There was a picture of Cormac on what was probably his first day of primary school in his mother's arms, which contrasted to the one next to it of James' first day with Cormac standing at his little brother's side. Cormac looked shy and nervous in his mother's embrace, overwhelmed by the slightly too big uniform, while James' seemed excited, with a smile that was big and toothy, his eyes filled with wonder.

Victoria noted each picture of Cormac with his parents was mirrored by one with Cormac and James as best as the older brother could remake it.

But it was a single picture, tucked away in the corner of the room on the bookcase, that made Victoria pause. Her eyes burned with a well of sudden emotion, her eyes blinking back the onset of unexpected tears that threatened to fall. In the picture, Cormac was dressed in his graduation garb, standing on his own in what appeared to be a school hall, diploma in hand. It wasn't a fancy formal shot clasping his certificate against a terrible backdrop as the ones Pippa and Hattie had. This was a quick photograph taken by someone else, probably a friend or a parent of a friend as Cormac tried to smile for them. In the background, she could see other students standing for such candid shots, but with others gathered around them, hugging and squealing in delight, no doubt.

Victoria found herself reaching up and tracing her finger over the young man's face. He'd lost his parents just six weeks before this day and his only living relative was still in an incubator in a hospital a fifty-mile drive away. While his friends were cheering and squealing around him, bragging about the futures they each had open to them, Cormac was already carrying the weight of the world. So, while his smile was wide and beaming, it didn't reach his eyes. Their green depths screamed sadness and longing, of a wish buried in them she knew only too well, as she'd had a similar desire after her mother had passed.

She wanted to wrap her arms around the younger man, hold him and tell him he'd do brilliantly. That he'd take care of his brother, keeping him loved, fed, and educated. James was a happy and carefree six-year-old and his parents would be proud of him…

'Do you take milk and sugar?' Cormac's shout made Victoria jump, and she quickly pulled her hand away from the lonely image. She resisted the urge to march into the kitchen and do exactly what she'd just imagined.

'Touch of milk, please,' she called back, heading towards the doorway, meeting him as he came in with two non-matching mugs in his hands. Victoria raised her brow as he handed one to her, but smiled politely as she took a sip, refraining from wincing as she realised it had been made from a teabag.

Cormac fell heavily onto the small couch and looked up at her over the rim of his mug as he took a gulp of his drink. His eyes travelled over her body, lingering on her tiny breasts, and Victoria felt her nipples tighten into buds under his scrutiny. His eyes darkened with desire and she watched his tongue sweep over his lips before pulling his lower one between his teeth and biting down.

'Are you going to just stand there?' he finally asked, his voice once again deep and gruff.

'You haven't invited me to sit, yet,' Victoria said, her own voice husky with desire. His cheeks flushed red at the polite correction to his manners, and he quickly mumbled his apologies.

'Oh, right, yeah,' he stuttered as he made to stand up. 'Lady and all that. Please, take a seat.' He waved his hand to the place beside his and waited for her to sit before taking his own seat again. Victoria noted his attempt to inconspicuously adjust his trousers and had to bite back her own smile.

She lowered her gaze to hide the gleam of triumph in her eyes as she began to believe this was going to go better than she'd dared hoped.

'Thank you,' she said with a polite smile as she glanced around for somewhere to put the heavy mug.

'You don't have to do this,' he said, taking the mug from her hand and popping it on the floor at the side of the sofa. 'I don't expect royal visits so the neighbours know what I've done. So long as you're safe and well, that's all fine and dandy.'

A warm feeling settled within her chest at his humility. In her social standing, a commendation would be expected. Hell, if she hadn't mentioned their actions to her grandfather for recognition from him, *her* name would be mud.

'I see,' Victoria said, shifting slightly in her seat to take him in properly. He gazed down at his cup, his fingers playing at the side of the rim. He was as uncomfortable with her presence as she was being in such a place, and the elation she'd been feeling just a moment ago quickly dwindled away.

She'd been looking at this rather one-sided. Could she make him comfortable in her world? She certainly knew she'd never be comfortable in his... Would she?

She glanced around the room with new eyes, trying to imagine it with different furnishings, lighter and brighter paint on the walls, some new curtains, cleaned windows... It would still be small, the outside would still be an almost apocalyptic wasteland, but the flat itself wouldn't be *too* bad, she supposed. But, and this was the thought that kept nagging her, she wouldn't be allowed to resign herself to this lifestyle and if she could elevate Cormac and his brother, surely they'd take that offer. It wasn't as if he'd have to be in her social circle often. After all, once she got her money, she aimed to step back as much as she possibly could. Perhaps the two of them could find a new social circle, maybe somewhere in the middle where they could both fit in?

She glanced behind Cormac to the bookcase again, taking in the textbooks that lined its shelves. They weren't the reading material of someone satisfied with their lot in life. Her eyes flicked back to Cormac's graduation picture. What had he planned on doing with his life before his parents had died and he'd become the sole guardian of his brother?

'Mr Blake—'

'Please, call me Cormac.'

'Cormac, I am incredibly grateful for your assistance last Wednesday evening-'

'Like I said, you're welcome.'

'Yes, I understand.' She bit back her frustration at once more being interrupted, and instead fixed her gaze firmly on him. Time to get straight to the point then.

'Cormac, you said if I ever needed rescuing again, I need only to call.'

When he raised his eyes to meet hers, she saw the curiosity she'd expected, but there was also a hint of hesitancy, almost a caution in his eyes that he didn't know how to hide.

She should have anticipated that, but it also reminded her how much of an open book he was, something she'd have to work on with him if he were to survive her relatives, even for a short amount of time.

'Are you okay?' he asked, sitting forward, putting his own mug down as he reached for her. He took her hand in his and held it tight. 'Is that Simon guy causing you more trouble?'

She shook her head with an endeared smile upon her lips. She was touched by his reaction, of his desire to protect, and in that moment, Victoria knew she'd made the right decision in approaching him. No matter what was thrown at them later, he would protect her as best he could.

'No,' she assured him, putting her other hand atop his. 'Simon has already confessed to his crimes and faces judgement tomorrow at the Broken Hill. Marcus says he'll face at least thirty years for the charges against him.'

Cormac let out a low whistle at the information, his hand relaxing under hers, but he made no move to pull away.

'Man, that's good to hear,' he said with a nod of his head. 'What were the charges?'

'Um…' She bit the inside of her cheek as she tried to remember the list Marcus had given her. She couldn't remember every one but the big three would suffice.

'Attempted kidnapping, attempted sexual assault, and bodily harm with a narcotic.'

'And that only gets him thirty years?'

'At *least* thirty, unless I give my good grace to him.'

'And will you? Speak up for him?' He asked, and Victoria shook her head. 'Good.' He said it so forcefully, Victoria looked up at him in surprise. 'What he did was abhorrent; the bastard deserves everything he gets and then some.'

Silence fell between them for a moment as Victoria considered the man who had allowed them to meet. Alexi had been wracked with guilt by the whole thing and none of them knew why he'd done it. Even Marcus couldn't get an answer from him. Although, Hattie's colorful conclusion of *the only way the fat bastard could get laid* seemed to be the reason everyone was favouring right now.

'So how can I help?' Cormac finally asked.

'I… I have a… *proposal* for you. As you may know, my father died recently-'

'I'm sorry to hear that,' Cormac spoke over her again, but the reassuring squeeze of her hand and the genuine understanding in his eyes made Victoria instantly forgive him; losing parents was a sorrow they both shared.

'Well,' she caught herself before she lowered her gaze. 'My father left me quite a substantial fortune, but there are certain *stipulations* within the will that must be met before

I'm able to gain access to my fortune and be completely independent from the Crown.

'As you are probably aware from my little... *display* last week, I'm not overly fond of my grandfather being part of my life. I would like to access my inheritance as quickly as possible to remove myself from my royal obligations, and I'm willing to offer you a deal if you help me meet the requirements.'

Cormac frowned, shifting in his seat, and carefully pulled his fingers from her grasp. A wary look came over his face. She had to bite back the mew of frustration, knowing that this may not go over as easily as she'd dared to hope. 'And they are?'

'I won't gain a single penny of my cut of the money unless I get married before I'm thirty-five, which I happen to turn in September.' She hoped he'd get her meaning, that he'd understand what she was asking him, without her *actually* asking, but the man simply continued to stare at her with his beautiful green eyes.

'Which is just over ten weeks away.' When he still said nothing, Victoria took a deep breath.

'Cormac Dean Blake, I'm asking you to *marry* me.'

∽

MARRY HER? AS IN HAVE A WEDDING? BECOME HER *HUSBAND*?

Bonded in holy matrimony? Till death them do part?

No, she hadn't asked that... She *couldn't* have asked that. Right?

'I'll pay you, of course,' Victoria hastened to add, bobbing her head quickly as if that made the question any better. 'I'll give you twenty percent of my share of the inheritance. Marry me and I'll make you rich beyond your wildest dreams...'

Cormac stared at Victoria who looked back at him expectantly. She had a small, hesitant smile curling her lips and her high cheekbones held a hint of pink to them as she waited for his response, hope lighting her eyes. But as the silence lingered, that light slowly faded, and the corners of her mouth flattened before turning downward. She cleared her throat as the silence moved from understandable to uncomfortable, and the pink of her cheeks became a brighter red that filled her face.

Cormac watched, unable to move, think, or speak as the flush quickly travelled down her neck to the top of her chest, which rose and fell with deep breaths. The image of her chest rising and falling from other activities sprang to mind, as he thought of her laid out on their marital bed.

Would that be part of the bargain? Would he get to share her bed of a night, sample that peachy skin, nuzzle between those perfect little breasts as he slowly made his way down her body? Would her legs part for him, open and inviting, letting him seek the reward he wanted most? How would she react? Would her back arch in pleasure as her fingers gripped the sheets, or would she grab at his hair, holding him in place as she ground herself against his face, working in time with his tongue—

'Yes, well.' Her clipped tone jarred him from his thoughts, and he felt his own face flush, hoping she wouldn't see the reaction he'd had to the idea of them together, entwined in the most intimate of ways—

She stood quickly, smoothing down the front of her dress, and before he could say anything, she turned and made to grab the small bag she'd tucked behind her.

'Victoria…' His voice was a soft murmur, warm and rich, as he reached out to grab her wrist and stop her. He had a million questions on his lips, but they fell away when he saw the file with his own name written on it in thick black pen tucked next to her bag.

'What's this?' His hand reached over hers and grabbed at

the folder, snatching it from her fingertips. He flipped it open, and several loose photographs fell from its confines. He frowned as he realised it was him in his car stuck at the side of the road when the damn piece of shit had got a flat on his way to work a week ago. Another image showed his frustration, kicking the car as he failed to remove the wheel. A third painted a pitiful picture of him as he sat in the gutter, his head in his hands as he had a brief moment of despair when he'd decided to just give up and pack it all in, send James off to one of the boarding homes, and run as far as he could from all his problems… And then finally, a shot of him once he'd picked himself back up and started again, this time getting the damn wheel off and the spare on in its place.

He flicked through the stack of other photographs. He didn't think he had this many of him throughout his *life*. But here there were dozens and dozens; him at the gym, at work, at the supermarket, picking up James from—

'You took photographs of my brother?' He glared up at her frozen form. 'He's six years old and this is at his *school*! He's supposed to be safe there…' He ground his teeth, holding back his outrage. He wanted to scream and shout; she had no right to do this! He didn't care how beautiful she was, how rich she and her family were, or that they were connected to the King. She didn't have the *right* to invade his life, his *privacy* like this.

He paused, looking at the photo more carefully.

'You… This was the day *after* I saved your arse!' he said, jumping up from his seat and thrusting the picture in her face. Victoria leaned back but didn't step away. She plucked the photograph from his grasp, only to have it replaced by his finger. 'Did you have someone following me immediately? Think I was part of some elaborate scheme to kidnap you? Perhaps you figured I set it up just so I could rescue you and get some money or a title or some other thing you royals like to give out—'

'Mr Blake, please, don't be so ridiculous—

'Ridiculous? You think I'm being *ridiculous* when I've basically had my life hacked for the last week or so?'

'We didn't hack you; you have no online presence. How do you live without at least an *email* address?'

'Don't push it, princess,' he growled, taking a step towards her. Again, she refused to move, to yield to him; it infuriated him further and, confusingly, endeared her to him. This was a woman, who despite their meeting, didn't allow others to walk all over her. She was going to fight for what she wanted and apparently, that was him. Her small breasts pressed against his chest, and he had to will his hands to remain clenched at his side and not wrap them around her waist and pull her tight against him before he claimed her mouth.

He had itched to have her in his arms again from the moment he'd opened the door to her. He'd dreamt of her almost every night since they'd met, always starting with him rescuing her from ludicrous situations and ending with her giving him her eternal thanks... His favourite thanks was her sliding down his body from a similar position to the one they were in now, and slowly opening his trousers and teasing him as she-

'Mr Blake, I apologise for having you investigated, but I had to know if I could trust you. If there were—*are*—any skeletons in your closet that could come back and bite me in the behind'—he rolled his eyes at her polite phrases—'and expose me to my grandfather or even my father's enemies.'

The image of Conner O'Malley, sitting smoking his cigar, flashed through Cormac's mind. His stomach dropped as he recalled the deal he'd agreed to on Tuesday night.

'I had to do this to check that you weren't on drugs or addicted to gambling and in a heap load of debt-' She cut herself off on the word *debt*, wincing at her own slip of her tongue and he knew she was aware of how weak his financial position was. He wasn't in a *heap load*, but he couldn't afford to keep going. 'I had to know what liabilities you carried before I knew if I could ask for your help.'

'By proposing to me?' He shook his head as he turned and stepped away from her, putting some space between them to try and calm the confusing rush of emotions taking over his body. 'I don't get it; why are you proposing to *me*? Look, princess-'

'Not a princess.'

'Lady, whatever. My point is, you must have a dozen or so suitors out there you could propose to, someone more of your standing.'

'I've tried dating those types of men—I believe you met one of them last Wednesday.' He froze in his step, his head snapping towards her at her words. She raised her brow at the point and Cormac grimaced at the memory of seeing the woman before him unconscious, completely at the mercy of the sicko and anyone else the bastard had wanted to hand her over to. The mere thought made him sick to his stomach.

The thought of anyone being in such a situation was disgusting, but recalling *her* in that position did something to him. A raw, instinctual need to just reach out and gather her up, hide her away from the world and protect her from everyone and everything. He stopped in front of her and reached out, without thinking, tracing his fingers down her cheek to reassure himself she was still there. Her breath hitched at his touch, and she turned into it ever so slightly. Her eyes fell closed, and her tongue slipped over her slightly parted lips to wet them before disappearing once more, making him want to chase it.

Cormac swallowed at the image she portrayed; sweet and innocent, and he felt that basic instinct to protect her rise again.

But to *marry* her…

'You saved my life, Cormac,' she told him, her voice barely more than a murmur as she opened her eyes and gazed up at him through her long, dark lashes, truth and conviction shimmering within them. 'Of that I have no doubt, and yet, knowing who I was, you didn't seek me out for recompense or a reward-'

'Of course not,' he said, snatching his hand back. He couldn't touch her, couldn't be lured into whatever she was offering him by his libido, or influenced by her womanly charms. His mind was already whirling, trying to figure out how to tell O'Malley about her visit without telling him *exactly* what she'd offered.

'Who the hell looks for something like that?' he asked, his voice far gruffer than he'd heard before. 'I mean, you were hurt, vulnerable... Anyone would have done the same without expecting anything in return.'

She gazed at him with big, sad, brown eyes and her lush mouth curled up on one side into a forlorn little smile that he just wanted to kiss.

'You'd be surprised.' Her voice was soft, sorrowful, and that thing inside him, the thing he couldn't put a finger on deep within his core sent his protective male instincts into overdrive. The need to gather her up, pull her to him and never let her go reared its head again, and Cormac made a frustrated grunt as he turned away once more.

This was insane. Things like this, princesses turning up to propose to strippers, just didn't happen in real life. A stray thought crossed his mind, wondering if O'Malley had suspected what Lady Victoria was going to *propose* to him. He'd seemed very smug when he'd mentioned her offering Cormac something, very self-assured... Was there someone feeding O'Malley information on the woman before him? Someone in the royal house?

'My sisters and I,' she continued to explain, and Cormac mused if the spy could be one of her sisters. 'Have been searching high and low for a man who will treat me well throughout the marriage without stepping on me, without commanding me, without thinking he *owns* me in some way—'

'So, you just want to own *me?*' He said the words without thinking.

'No,' she said vehemently. He heard two small steps to reach him and glanced down at the hand on his bicep as she tried to get him to look at her. Against his better judgement, he turned to her and met her earnest eyes.

'That's the point. I don't want anyone to *own* anyone in this marriage. I want a clear arrangement. From your actions the other night—and from what I've read in your dossier—I feel that you're a man who always keeps a level head about him even in the worst situations.'

He wanted to snort at that comment. If she knew what had been going on inside his head this past week, the worry about money, the guilt every time the unwelcome idea of giving his brother up popped into his head, and the sheer loneliness at his situation, she'd not only take those words back, but run a mile too.

He wondered what she'd say if he told her what O'Malley had offered her…

His mind stopped on that thought.

He *could* tell her what O'Malley wanted. He could reveal that there was someone in her inner circle—maybe that Marcus?—in touch with her father's competition. Of course, she'd probably storm out, leaving him with nothing, contacting O'Malley and telling him to back off. Then O'Malley would fire his arse and he'd be right back to where he was last night before he'd called his grand-boss. He rubbed his temples, trying to work out what to do.

If he said no and told O'Malley, she'd find out from the leak and then he'd have the Royal Guard on him, causing him nightmares. If he said no and told O'Malley something else, he might get fired because Cormac was sure the guy *knew* what she was offering him. He couldn't say she'd never been because O'Malley probably already knew she was here, hell, the guy was probably watching *him*.

His only option was to say yes and tell O'Malley where to go… But then O'Malley would probably tell Victoria that Cormac had accepted to squeal on her and she'd dump his arse. He'd end up right back where he was last night with no job, no money, and a different difficult decision to make.

'Cormac, I need a husband, a name on a piece of paper, to satisfy the stipulations of the will. We can look at it as a joint business venture if you'd prefer. Marry me, in the next two months, help me produce an heir within the next five years, and, in return, I will give you twenty-five-'

'An *heir!*' He reeled back, pulling himself away from her touch.

Victoria physically winced at his reaction, and hurried to add, 'I should have mentioned that sooner, but yes, an heir is required as part of the conditions.'

She wanted kids? With him, a complete and total failure? A joke of a man? He wanted to laugh, to ask her who the hell had compiled that file on him because they'd clearly missed all that. And how the hell could he have a kid with her when he was trapped in this fucking *deal* with the devil?

'Bloody hell, princess! Why don't you just… just'—he waved his hand around as he tried to think of an alternative solution—'ask a gay friend? Or get some sperm from one of those clinics; why even the whole façade of getting married?'

'I told you, the will has specific clauses,' she admitted with a sigh as she ran her hands over her face before dropping them to her sides. He suddenly realised that behind the make-up, she looked tired and the slump of her shoulders spoke of defeat.

Geri's blue-haired face popped into his head and the memory of her ranting over an article about Lady Victoria the day after the attack rang loud and clear in his ear.

She'd gone on about how unfair it was that the media

were practically hunting her down since she'd come out to play. When he'd asked what she meant, Geri had explained how the woman before him had always been quite reclusive, but she'd suddenly become the talk of the town by dating a new man almost every other night since her father's death. The gossip columns were touting that while her father was alive, he'd forbidden her from dating and now she was sowing her royal oats. Others said she was being forced to marry by her grandfather; as the eldest of the royal grandchildren, she had to marry before any of the others could be walked down the cathedral's aisle.

Now Cormac knew the truth, and with the way she looked up at him imploringly, he wondered if *he* was her last chance. What would she do if he denied her? Would she be thrust into her grandfather's hands? Would he *force* her to marry? Would she even get a say in it?

The idea of her being frogmarched down the aisle to some foreign prince made him feel sick. She might as well have been left to that Simon for all the difference it would make. He'd rescued her from such a fate once; was he willing to do it again—permanently?

'I have to be married to the father of my heir,' she continued as his mind whirled at a hundred miles per hour. 'And said heir has to be produced *naturally*. No IVF, no adoptions, no fostering…'

He swallowed. 'When you say *naturally*…?'

She paused, her mouth opening to speak, but no sound came out. The fingers still lightly gripping his arm flexed ever so slightly before she slowly withdrew it.

'I mean,' she said, and he knew she was picking her words carefully. 'The marriage will need to be… um…'—her face flushed bright red, and she stepped back; her hands moved nervously as she spoke—'*consummated*… to make it official. And… um, probably *frequently* if I'm… if I'm to *conceive* at my age.' She offered him a grimace of a smile as she stopped in her retreat.

'Frequently?' he said, not moving from where he stood. She nodded, that same grimace-smile on her face as she looked at him with beseeching eyes. She made a *mmhmm* noise as she nodded.

'Yes, after thirty, a woman's fertility tends to drop, and after thirty-five, which I'm approaching, the eggs become even less-'

Oh, God, no. He wasn't having *this* conversation. He held up his hand, his own wincing smile plastered across his face as she thankfully stopped speaking.

'Okay, yeah, I get it. Biological clock. Ticking. Okay.' He ran a hand through his hair as he took a deep breath. This wasn't something he'd thought he'd have to think about for a long time. Years, perhaps, until James was going off to university and he could finally put himself first…

'You did say if I needed any more help…' Her tentative tone made him scoff.

'Yeah, I meant, like if you needed a ride somewhere or a place to hide from your grandfather. Not be your husband and baby daddy.'

Victoria straightened her shoulders, her shoulders rolling back, and her chin lifting ever so slightly. Cormac saw The Lady Snape in all her magnanimous glory. She was beautiful, breathtaking. She could be his…

'I'm sorry, Mr Blake, you're absolutely right.' Her tone changed from nervous hope to all business in a heartbeat. 'What I am asking is far too much to ask of anyone. I apologise unreservedly for invading your privacy and taking your time today.' She turned, grabbing her handbag and the file he'd left on the sofa. 'Please forget that I ever called. I will inform the King of your heroic part in my mishap last week and he will ensure that you are well rewarded. I will, of course, destroy this.'

She held up the folder before tucking it under her arm.

The sudden change in attitude made his head spin. If she left right now, she'd go back and tell whoever was leaking the information that he'd turned her down and O'Malley would know.

Dammit, he needed more time!

'Whoa, hang on a moment there, princess.' It was his turn to reach out and gently take her elbow in his hand, turning her back to him and stopping her from moving. 'I never said I *wouldn't* do it-'

'You mean you will?' There was that hope in her eyes again.

'I never said that either.' He licked his lips as he tried to find the right words. 'Look, what you're asking of me isn't just *big*, it's freaking *enormous*! It's life-changing-'

'For the better, as I said, I'll make you very rich in your own right,' she hurried to add, and Cormac had to bite his lip to stop from reaching out and slapping a hand over her mouth.

'Princess, will you let me finish?' She instantly closed her mouth, rolling her lips together until there was just a thin line and she mimed pulling a zip across them. Cormac sighed as he looked down at her.

'I need some time to think this through. Weigh everything up. I don't just have myself to think about here. I've got James too.' Victoria nodded her head; her gaze softened but held a hint of sorrow. 'When do you need an answer by?'

'When I leave, the offer is off the table.'

'What?' Well, that wasn't going to do.

'I can't have you discussing this with someone while you make up your mind and the rules of the will getting out somehow.'

His heart picked up pace at her words, trying to claw its way into his mouth as he imagined standing in front of

O'Malley and telling him she'd proposed to him to claim her fortune.

'Are you… Are you not allowed to do that?'

'No, that's not it. But imagine if people knew what getting married meant for me and my sisters? How would we ever know who really loved us and who was just after the money?'

'But you're not marrying for love.'

Victoria shook her head. 'No, I'm not, but my sisters still have a chance to.' She paused, hesitating on what she wanted to say before she took a breath and continued. 'Once upon a time, I thought I would marry for love. I'd meet a dashing man who would sweep me off my feet, we'd move into a lovely home and raise half a dozen babies, but I've come to accept that's not my lot in life. I then tried to find someone I could have companionship with, but even that has been difficult.

'Mr Blake, if you don't agree today, then I am submitting to the will of my grandfather who, no doubt, will pack me off to mainland Europe and start to parade me around the royal houses there.' She tucked her hair behind her ear as she sighed. Her eyes dropped from his to where his feet were firmly planted on the ugly carpet.

'If I lost my fortune, that I could come to terms with. Sure'—she shrugged—'I'd be dependent on my sisters for a while, but I could cope while I learnt to support myself. But my grandfather would never allow it. He wants Alistair to marry and produce heirs, and he can't until I'm led down the aisle first… Stupid traditions.'

So, Geri's magazines were right—not that he'd ever tell his little smurfy-friend so.

'And if I say yes?' Her eyes snapped back to his.

'If you say yes, I have a car outside that will immediately take the two of us to *Cartwright, Daven, Mercer, and Associates* where I have an appointment in'—she checked her watch

—'an hour and twenty minutes to sign one of two documents.'

Cormac rubbed his hand over his mouth, feeling the bristles that came with a day of not shaving. His mind and heart were at war with one another; his head screaming that this was stupid, insane, and so utterly beyond the realm of normalcy, he should start checking for hidden cameras. But his heart...

His heart was looking down at this woman and telling him to say *yes*. There were no arguments being bounced along its rhythm. No counterpoints between its beats. Just a simple thump of *yes, yes, yes* as it pattered in his chest as Victoria stared at him.

However, he was a hundred percent on board with his brain; this *was* crazy. No one in their right mind would agree to marry someone they didn't know, that they'd met only once... Even if they were the most beautiful woman they'd ever seen. That every time he looked into her eyes, his heart began to pound in his chest, his hands itched to reach out and just touch her, and his arms longed to gather her to him and hold her tight.

And then there was O'Malley to consider too...

No, this was just insane, absolutely-

The letterbox on the door slammed down over and over and James' small shouts of *Cormac* through it snapped him from his daze.

'James, stop that!' he bellowed, leaning around Victoria to call into the hallway. 'Gimme a minute.'

He took a second to look around the grotty, little room he both slept and lived in. The peeling wallpaper that lined the walls, the vile carpet that curled at the edges of the room, and the tiny table that held a pile of bills...

He'd not slept all night, tossing and turning on the sofa-bed as his mind whirled over what the hell O'Malley's threat had meant. But the guy had made good on his promise to transfer him enough money to cover the eviction; he'd called his bank first thing, and the money was there. It was gone again a few minutes later when he'd sent the payment to his landlord.

'Corrie! C'mon, I need to *wee!*' James' voice called again, and Cormac could easily picture his brother hopping from one foot to the other as he held himself. He was always leaving it until he burst, probably explained the bed-wetting a little.

He swung himself around again to the waiting Lady.

'Just... gimme a moment,' he said, holding up one finger and moving out into the hallway.

His brain was no longer screaming at him. In fact, it had gone noticeably quiet as it tried to work out if its initial evaluation was completely correct. As he opened the door and a flurry of colour raced through the small parting and whizzed by into the tiny mould-infested bathroom, his brain decided it was absolutely one hundred percent right; it *was* completely insane. *But* that didn't mean it wouldn't benefit him.

Marrying her *would* solve everything. He'd be able to keep James with him, his debts would be cleared, he'd have a chance to make something of himself, and he'd almost certainly be able to get James into the gifted programme...

His only issue was what to do with O'Malley.

He heard the toilet flush and knew he only had a moment before his brother reappeared.

Cormac stepped into the doorway and saw Victoria still standing in the middle of the room, looking so out of place in a dress that probably cost more than a month's rent of their crappy home. She tried to look nonchalant, as if her fate wasn't resting in the hands of a stranger, but her fidgeting fingers gave her away. Their eyes met for a moment before something at his side caught her attention.

'Who are you?' James' curious voice asked with all the aplomb only a six-year-old could have.

'James,' Cormac said, his eyes fixed on the woman standing in their home, looking so out of place. His hand reached down and rested on his brother's shoulder as he said, 'I'd like you to meet her Ladyship, Lady Victoria, my fiancée.'

CHAPTER NINE

To anyone looking at the scene, Victoria was engaged in a conversation with her driver while the two Blake brothers were having a quiet, yet heated discussion a few steps away. However, Victoria's attention was firmly on the two men that were about to become her family, and Toby knew it. It was a trick Victoria had learnt a long time ago, and it had served her well over the years.

The older woman—a Mrs Battersea, Cormac had called her—stood on the bottom step of the stairs that led up to Cormac's tiny flat, and unlike Victoria, she had no such compunction to make it look as if she wasn't listening intently to Cormac and James.

Cormac had explained to her, before he'd dashed out to knock on the woman's door and beg her assistance, that their elder neighbour had babysat for James when Cormac was at work, and Victoria had been eager to meet the woman who was really the only mother figure in James' life. Victoria's smile had been genuine when the woman had stepped inside the living room, but it quickly became her practised smile of politeness when Mrs Battersea had recovered from the shock of seeing her standing in Cormac's living room and openly *glared* at Victoria.

As Victoria had watched the woman, settling in the tiny living room as Cormac ran and got changed, a sense of familiarity had grown. Victoria was certain they'd never met before, but her features reminded her of someone, and it made Victoria uneasy for reasons she couldn't put her finger on. It threw up alarm bells that Marcus had drilled into her years ago and they were already on high alert after last week.

She made a mental note to ask Marcus for a full report on the woman later.

'—but *when* did you get a girlfriend?' James asked, unable —or unwilling—to let go of the conversation as Cormac kept asking him to. 'You're always either working or with *me*. Did you meet her at work?'

Victoria coughed, choking on the air in her lungs at the thought of working in such a place… or attending as a customer. Her grandfather would have a heart attack at the mere idea of her being in the vicinity of such an establishment, and she was still surprised that he hadn't contacted her regarding the news story last week. It had run in several newspapers and appeared on both the breakfast news and the news at six on all but the state-run Avalonian Broadcasting Network, so he *must* have seen it… Unless Marcus had pulled off a miracle.

'James, you're six; this isn't something you need to worry about. We're going to go and live in a nice place, and have nice things and, maybe, you'll go to a better school.'

He could count on it, Victoria thought, and added a viewing of Highbourne Academy to her ever-growing to-do list. She hadn't been back to it since her own school days and she was mildly interested in how much it must have changed over the years. Large donations from the wealthy—all trying to get their children in that didn't make the grade—tended to rapidly improve the facilities. From what little there was to learn about James, it was clear she wouldn't have to make any such donations. Even if that weren't the case, she was sure having the first royally connected child in over a decade attending would ensure his placement in September—even if they were extremely late in applying.

'Ma'am.' Toby gently interrupted her thoughts. 'If we're to make your next appointment, we need to get moving.'

'Of course, Toby,' she said with a small nod. She pasted on her royal-occasion serene smile and turned back to the two Blake brothers.

'I'm terribly sorry to interrupt,' she said just as James opened his mouth to reply to Cormac. 'But we must be leaving.' She glanced down at the pink-gold and diamond Cartier watch to emphasise her point.

'Look, I'll be back later, okay.' Cormac crouched down to be at eye level with James as he said goodbye. 'I want you to go through your things and start to think about what you want to keep so we can pack them away-'

'Yeah, I know how to do *that*.' James rolled his eyes and turned away from his older brother, dragging his feet as he slowly walked towards the steps over which his babysitter stood guard.

'We won't be long,' Cormac called to him as he stood up. James didn't look back, but gave a half-hearted wave over his shoulder as he trudged up the steps. Mrs Battersea shook her head as she watched the younger brother until he turned and disappeared.

'He'll be fine,' the older woman reassured Cormac with a smile before she narrowed her eyes and finished with, 'Just make sure *you* are.'

Cormac's shoulders rose and fell before turning back to Victoria, a lop-sided smile on his face. 'I guess my carriage awaits.' He tried to joke, but his heart clearly wasn't in it. Victoria nodded and gracefully climbed in the car, suddenly distracted by doubt. Was this the right choice? Had Kirstie been right to dismiss the idea out of hand?

She'd considered everything from *her* point of view, but what about Cormac's? All she'd seen were the positives; getting him out of debt, moving him into a better place, giving him the opportunities he'd been denied by his parents' death and the subsequent raising of his younger brother. She'd thought about the doors that would open for James as he grew up, attending the best schools the country had to offer. She'd thought he could grow up to become a doctor or a lawyer, maybe an engineer or scientist… She hadn't thought about the fact that they might be leaving friends behind. That they might not hold the same ideas or aspirations that she did.

'What do you want?' she blurted out the words the moment the door closed behind Cormac. 'I mean,' she started again, composing herself. He hadn't even settled into the seat, and she was already demanding things of him. 'I've been very up front in what I need from you and what I'm offering you for that.'

'Yeah, twenty-percent of whatever you inherit,' he mumbled.

The driver's door of the car opened, and Victoria quickly pressed a button, turning the divider between the front and rear of the vehicle from transparent to opaque, giving them complete privacy.

'Do you know how much that is?' When he didn't answer, his fingers nervously playing with the seatbelt, Victoria added, 'That's twenty-five *million* crowns, Cormac.' She let the number sink in. Watched as his head slowly rose and his eyes met hers. A myriad of emotions flickered within his green eyes. 'As long as I reach *all* the conditions of the will.'

'And what if we don't? What if we can't'—he waved his hand between the two of them—'you know?'

'Have sex?' A pink blush filled his cheeks, and Victoria's smile grew wide. There was such a sweetness, an innocence to the man, and it made her want to just snuggle up next to him.

She made a mental note to ensure her cousins didn't get too close to her future husband. They'd rip him to shreds and laugh over his remains. The bloody vultures.

The small wisp of arousal, that had lingered within her ever since Cormac had opened the door to her, grew, curling deliciously upwards, warming her as his eyes drifted over her body, lingering on her thigh where the skirt of her dress had ridden up to reveal the bottom of the lace of her stockings.

This was the biggest personal obstacle they'd have to overcome. Class and etiquette could be taught, and they could build a friendship over time to make the marriage bearable, but sex between them…

She'd worried it might be a cold impersonal thing, that she'd have to lie back and think of Avalone, while he closed his eyes and imagined someone else beneath him, but from the way his eyes lingered on her body, the way he had shifted earlier to try and hide his own attraction to her, she thought sex might actually be something *very* enjoyable between them.

'I don't think I'll have a problem there,' she whispered, her voice dropping slightly as she gazed up at him through her lashes. 'Do you?'

He licked his lips as he stared back at her and slowly shook his head.

'No,' he said, his voice far deeper than before. 'But, er, what I meant was, what if we can't, you know, have children?' He wasn't the most articulate, she surmised, but he had a good point, and she wanted to praise him for asking the right questions.

'Then I get nothing. *But,*' she hastened to add as a dawning horror crept over his face and he made to speak. 'We'll have five whole years from our wedding day to try. During that time, I will get a monthly stipend and I will ensure that there is a *substantial* amount put aside for you from that as a fall-back just in case.' She gracefully reached for her handbag from beside her feet and searched for her compact and lipstick. When she found them, she glanced towards Cormac who was stared at her, frowning.

'But if there's something else you'd like? I mean, whatever I can do to make this easier on you. And James.'

'I want him in a good school-'

'I was thinking Highbourne Academy.' She opened the compact and twisted her lipstick up. 'Usually, admissions for the new school year are sorted well before now, but I'm *sure* they'll be begging for James as soon as they see his scores.'

'I also want James taken care of. If this doesn't work out, I want it guaranteed that he'll have his education provided all the way through university, that he won't go hungry or cold again, and that he'll always have a proper roof over his head, even if...'

She paused mid-application of her lipstick, stunned by his words. She had known they weren't in a good place, but exactly how bad had their situation been? How often had the pair gone without food or heat? The report did say the duo had lived in several addresses over the years, but she hadn't considered that perhaps they'd been moving *down* rather than *along* the property ladder.

'Even if what?' she probed, the compact in her hand dropping to her lap forgotten as she realised he'd trailed off. His lips closed shut and his eyes downcast as a frown marred his face. Cormac took a deep breath through his nose, unwilling to meet her gaze.

'Even if I can't be with him, even if it means I have to give up parental rights to him, I won't have him shown he can have everything only to have it snatched away again.'

Victoria didn't know what to say, or how to react. She couldn't believe he'd give up his brother just to ensure James had access to things she'd taken for granted over the years.

Victoria sat back in her seat and really took in the man at her side.

She'd always considered herself a good person. She knew her position came with privilege and she'd tried to never abuse it, never hold it over someone, to be the face of charities and good causes to encourage others to think about them, donate to them... But she'd never actually *thought* about the people being benefited by them. People like Cormac, someone who was so good at heart, he'd saved her life and never even thought of the chance of reward, even though he was on the verge of losing everything.

Or people in a more dire situation. She merely showed up at some fancy event, smiled and waved, gave a little prepared speech sent over by the charity that Kirstie would tweak, and then patted herself on the back for helping people as she was chauffeured back to her life of luxury at Renfrew Hall.

'Cormac,' she said slowly. 'Just how bad *is* your current situation? Say I hadn't made you this offer; how would you have been coping in a week or a month? Where would you be next year?'

'I— I had a little bit of luck recently.' He dropped his gaze from hers and plucked at the fabric of his jeans. 'My boss heard about my rent arrears and paid them off for me this morning as a thank you for doing my civic duty by rescuing you.'

'Wow,' Victoria said, her smile slowly returning. 'That's... That's great! Is that why you didn't seek me out?'

Cormac shook his head. 'No, no. I wasn't expecting it. He just told me last night and sent me the money this morning. I sorted it all out with my landlord just before you arrived.'

'Oh, I am glad.'

'But...' He trailed off and stared at the divider in front of them. Victoria could see he was carefully considering his words.

'Cormac, you can tell me, there's no shame in being in whatever position you were in.'

He cast her a disbelieving look, but took a deep breath and said, 'If he hadn't given me that money, then in a week I'd have been homeless—my landlord had sent me an eviction notice recently—and if I couldn't find a place within a few days, social services would have removed James. In a month, I'd have been living in my car, and in a year...' He let out a dry bark of a laugh that held no amusement. 'I'd have probably been on the streets somewhere, if I wasn't dead.'

Victoria swallowed. She didn't doubt the truth in his words. When she spoke, her words were but a whisper.

'Then I'm glad I made this choice, despite those against it.'

'Me too, princess.'

This time, she didn't correct him. Instead, she reached out and put her hand over his fidgeting fingers. He held on so hard, like a drowning man struggling to cling to life, Victoria thought as they raced through the streets towards their future.

She'd ensure he never had to step foot in water again, never mind keep his head above it.

∼

'THE SOLICITOR WE'RE ABOUT TO MEET, MR DAVEN, IS supposedly the best in the country,' Victoria began as soon as the lift doors slid shut and they began their quick ascent up into the heart of Avalone's tallest building, *The Heights*. 'I say supposedly because he was my father's solicitor but has never served the Crown.'

Of course, because her grandfather would snag all the best lawyers and doctors and whatnots for his own use, Cormac figured. Although, it wouldn't have surprised him for someone like Patrick Snape to bag the best and brightest for himself either. After all, rich people were all the same, title or not.

'Daven will know that this *isn't* a marriage for love, so we don't need to pretend to be romantic.' That was a bit of a relief, Cormac realised. It was one thing thinking of the mechanics of what they'd need to do, and another thinking of the emotional aspect. 'Of course, it's a different matter to the rest of the world.'

'The world?' he repeated.

She gazed up at him, her caramel eyes softening as she caught his confused expression.

'Well...' She sounded a little hesitant, as if she knew she was about to drop a bomb on him. *But what's one more?* his brain mocked. 'Even though I'm not a major member of the Royal Family, I *am* going to be the first of the King's grandchildren to get married. It will cause a bit of a storm here and, I imagine, around the world. As such, the King will surely be advised to make it a big deal which means he *will* make it into a big deal.'

'Wait,' Cormac interrupted. 'Is *he* going to be there?'

'Who? The King? Well, yes.'

Cormac's mind stuttered at that. He, Cormac Blake, a lowly, soon-to-be-unemployed ex-stripper was going to meet the King of Avalone? It sounded completely ridiculous. A tale in a silly romance novel—or a B-rated movie—not real life.

'If I wasn't the eldest of the royal grandchildren, I'd have got away with him not attending—his decision, of course. But as the one who always *had* to be the first to marry, he was always going to feature in the day. No matter my wishes. My sisters, of course, will be much luckier in that regard.'

'I have to meet the King.' His voice was barely a whisper. 'Shit.'

Victoria made to speak when the lift came to a stop and a *ping* sounded to say they had reached their destination. 'We'll talk about it later, just'—she pulled a grimace—'don't speak unless you have to and, please, think carefully about your choice of words. I have no idea who Daven reports to or where his loyalties lie.'

'Okay.' She must have heard the deflation in his voice, as she offered him a hint of a reassuring smile before her face changed again, smoothing out all emotion, her chin lifting ever so slightly as she pulled her shoulders back and stepped off the lift as the doors slid completely open. If Cormac hadn't seen her at her most vulnerable last week when confusion, fear, anger, bravery, and determination had raced through her, he'd have thought her a cold, heartless wretch. If he hadn't heard her plead—almost begging—with him that afternoon, he'd have assumed she thought herself above everyone with the way she held herself.

The couple—and that was a strange thought—walked the few paces towards the large ornate doors that were so intricately carved Cormac figured they probably cost more than his whole block of flats.

A man at the side of the doors stepped forward when Victoria stopped before them, and pushed the doors open before standing aside to let them through. Cormac noticed she didn't even acknowledge the doorman and wondered if she'd be like that every time they were in public. A sinking feeling within the pit of his stomach formed at such a thought.

The guy was probably no better off than Cormac was. He'd been a bellboy when James was just a baby, and lifting the heavy bags was a good workout for him when he couldn't afford the gym any longer. The doormen at the hotels he'd worked at had lived in tiny apartments, often alone after losing their spouses. It was a job they did thinking they'd meet people and not be so lonely any longer. People like Victoria—or at least the way she was acting—only seemed to exacerbate the loneliness with their high and mighty attitudes.

Would she expect him to act the same way?

She'd said they had a lot of work to do on him...

'Lady Snape,' a woman behind a desk, as ornate as the doors, said with a false warmth in her voice as she dipped her body slightly when Victoria approached her. Cormac resisted the urge to roll his eyes at the display. 'Mr Daven said to show you through immediately. Please, this way.'

They were led in silence down several corridors by the well-dressed receptionist before stopping outside of another set of double doors. These didn't have the intricate artwork of the entrance, but Cormac could still see they were solid wood, very heavy, and extremely expensive. He'd bet his left testicle they cost more than his rent for a year. Easily.

The woman knocked and without waiting for an answer, pushed open one of the heavy doors and ushered them inside.

'The Lady Snape and her... guest, sir,' the receptionist announced, her eyes sliding to Cormac as she emphasised the word *guest* as if waiting for him to correct her.

'Thank you, Roxanne. That will be all.' An old man struggled to his feet from behind a desk so large, Cormac reckoned at least ten people could fit around it. What the hell did someone do with a desk so big? The guy didn't even have a computer monitor on it!

'My lady.' The old solicitor dipped his head to acknowledge Victoria's status as she moved towards him and took a seat without waiting to be asked. Cormac, however, stood patiently, waiting to be acknowledged but it never came.

'Cormac, darling, come, join me.' Victoria patted the chair next to her as Mr Daven eased his elderly body back into his chair. Cormac wondered how old the man was—surely someone of his age should be retired by now?

'And who are you, boy?' the man snarled, glaring at Cormac over the rim of his glasses.

'You will address my fiancé with the same courtesy as you afford me,' Victoria snapped. The man's eyes slid from Cormac to the woman at his side, and Cormac saw the twitch in Daven's jaw as he bit back whatever words he really wanted to say to the woman before him.

Instead, he muttered, 'My apologies, ma'am.'

'Not to me, to *him*.'

The solicitor smiled, a twisted, reluctant thing before he turned to Cormac and offered him the smallest of nods he could get away with.

'We're playing the royal in full today, are we?' the solicitor asked as he sat back in his chair and assessed the pair, but his tiny eyes finally landed on Victoria. 'Far different from the last time we met.'

'The last time we met, I was in mourning.'

'Yes, and I have to say, you've recovered remarkably well and rather quickly.'

'Hey!' Cormac interrupted the man. 'Some people aren't able to take the time they need to mourn their losses properly. So, don't you-' Victoria's hand reached out to him, gently grasping at his forearm. He looked from the elegant, well-manicured hand up a slender arm, to Victoria's kind and gentle face. Her eyes spoke of understanding and gratitude at his comment, but her fingers flexing gently against his arm reminded him of where they were. He took a breath and sat back in his seat.

'Apologies,' he muttered, feeling the heat in his cheeks. They only burned hotter knowing he was going bright red. The other man continued to stare at him, and Cormac desperately tried not to squirm in his seat and failed.

'As I said, Cormac is my fiancé. I'm here to announce our intention to marry and complete the required paperwork to officially declare it.' She said it so matter-of-factly, it was almost as if it had always been the case. To give Mr Daven his due, he barely reacted. If his milky blue eyes hadn't briefly flickered to Cormac, Cormac would have wondered if the man had heard her at all.

'I haven't seen *him* in the papers,' the solicitor said.

'You've been keeping track of me.' It wasn't a question.

'I've kept abreast of your situation, yes,' Mr Daven agreed as he picked up a pen in his hand, avoiding her gaze.

'And my sisters?'

The man twirled the gold pen between his fingers and licked his shrivelled, dried lips, before answering. 'I am aware of certain things.'

Cormac wondered what those things where. He hadn't really thought about how Victoria's sisters were all in the same situation; were any of them involved with anyone? Would they be able to avoid having to go through what Victoria was having to do to secure her fortune? Although, with Victoria being the eldest, he assumed they'd have a lot more time than she'd been given.

'I see,' Victoria said, crossing her legs as she shifted in her seat and pressed her red painted lips together. Cormac could see she was debating saying something more, but it was a momentary thing, and, as if it made no difference to her what the man knew about her sisters, she proceeded with going through the legalities.

'While I don't have a legal mind, Mr Daven, I have read through the terms and conditions of the will repeatedly and at no point does it say that I must marry someone that I love.'

Her words seemed to intrigue the solicitor, who leaned forward, arms resting on the desk and his pen stilling in his hand. 'I don't think those words were used, no,' he agreed.

'As far as I understand it, the long and short of it is that I need to marry before I reach thirty-five and that said husband must sire a child with me, through natural means within five years of that marriage.'

'Yes.'

'Then Mr Blake here, has agreed to be my husband and to have children with me, if we're so blessed.'

'Has he now?' Mr Daven finally turned his gaze on Cormac.

'Um, yeah,' Cormac said, nodding his head.

'Now, regarding the Trust side of things.' Victoria ploughed on, not allowing the solicitor a chance to grill him or question the matter, for which Cormac was grateful. He had no idea how she was coming off as so relaxed about the whole thing; he just wanted to jump up and start shouting that this was madness, complete and utter madness! But listening to the two of them discussing the issue, it appeared completely normal; was this how things were done in their world? Were marriages still gateways to bigger fortunes and securing family names? Why the hell was he getting on board this train to crazy town?

'I have agreed to pay Cormac twenty percent of my inheritance in return for marrying me *and* siring a child with me.'

God, she made it sound so much like a transaction. Not that it was anything but, really. It didn't matter if he found her attractive—incredibly so—or if his hands itched to touch her, or that he was desperate to know what her kiss would taste like; this was all strictly business.

Still, it hurt to be discussed as if he were a stallion for sale. Prized or not.

'That's incredibly generous of you,' the solicitor said, finally putting the pen down and sitting up straight. He looked ten years younger the moment it became all business. Cormac admired that passion for something before the man turned his penetrating eyes on him, and he suddenly felt ten years old again, being called in front of the headmaster.

Cormac shifted in his seat guiltily. Did the solicitor know the deal he'd made with O'Malley? There had been no witnesses to hear their discussion. They'd only seen the two talking. And nothing was written down…

The older man narrowed his already tiny eyes at Cormac. 'Perhaps there's a *little* room for negotiation?'

Cormac had to stop himself from sighing with relief. He was focused on the money and to be fair, with the amount she'd told him he'd be worth after their marriage, Cormac knew she could have got him for less. *Twenty-five million crowns!* He'd almost fainted, hearing such a figure. He'd have done it for half the amount. Hell, she could have offered him a million *slivers,* and he'd have done it. As long as James was taken care of, that was all that mattered.

'No, there is no negotiation,' Victoria said firmly, before he could even open his mouth. 'That is what I offered as I feel that it is a fair price for Cormac to relinquish what could be up to five of the best years of his life. He's also having to give a part of himself to me, and, if I didn't think you'd have me put through the courts questioning my sanity, I'd have offered him fifty!'

'Million or percent?' Cormac asked, half joking, half serious. Victoria turned and he could see she was trying to bite back a smirk, knowing full well what he was doing.

'Percent,' she told him.

He whistled. 'That's a whole lot of crowns.'

'As is twenty-five million,' Mr Daven reminded them. His face was scrunched into a frown as he stared at Cormac across the desk.

'Quite.' Victoria agreed. 'Now, I need some paperwork drawing up that is very clear and easy to understand and can't be disputed in court. It clearly needs to state that Cormac and I are to marry and as long as I inherit my share of my father's estate, Cormac gets twenty percent of it.'

'Very well.' The solicitor picked his pen up again as he pulled a pad of paper towards him, but his eyes, filled with distrust, still lingered on Cormac.

'No hidden loopholes, nothing that entangles us in legal processes when I inherit,' she said, wagging her finger at the old man. Mr Daven finally turned his gaze to her, looking at her over the top of his glasses.

'Very well.' He scribbled down a few notes.

'I also want ten percent of my monthly stipend going directly into Cormac's account.' The solicitor's pen paused. Well, Cormac hadn't been expecting that either. He turned to Victoria to try and ask her what she was doing, but he saw her own eyes fixed on the man in front of her, daring him to say something or even look at her to challenge her request. Cormac wondered who the real Victoria was; the woman he'd rescued, who'd begged her ex-fiancé not to tell her grandfather of her ordeal, the one who'd pleaded with him to help her again, or the woman before him now, a no-nonsense take on the world, high-and-mighty princess who wouldn't back down from a fight. Maybe she was a bit of both.

Or—and he prayed this wasn't the case—maybe she was one of these women who'd switch her roles for the right person? A chameleon, an actress, a manipulator?

Cormac swallowed at the thought.

To give the solicitor his due, he didn't glance up. He merely asked *anything else* before jotting down another note.

'I looked through the terms of the stipend, and I'm entitled to housing, a car, *and* staff from the trust.' She ticked everything off on her fingers. 'I want a house somewhere in or near Earlsbury, somewhere easy enough for James to get to Highbourne Academy. Avon, as much as I'd like to stay here, isn't an option. It's an hour away and not fair for James to be travelling so much each day. And he's far too young for me to consider boarding him there.' Again, the solicitor paused.

'And just who is this *James*?'

'My younger brother,' Cormac answered. The solicitor sat up straight again and stared at Cormac. 'He's six, I'm his legal guardian. Our parents died when he was a week old, and I've been taking care of him ever since.' Something in the old man's eyes softened for a moment before it was once more hidden.

'I see.'

'Of course, the trust will pay for James' schooling.' Victoria wasn't asking a question.

'The trust is there to see to your spending needs. If you need your new brother-in-law to attend the finest academy in the country, that is what will happen.'

'I do.'

Mr Daven leaned forward and pressed a button on the phone on the table.

'Maya, please bring in the Intention to Marry Announcement forms.' He then turned back to Cormac and Victoria. 'We'll fill these in and sign them, and I will arrange the rest for you to sign at the end of next week. Do you have a date for the wedding in mind?' he enquired as a woman walked in with a stack of forms.

'Saturday, 29th August; seven weeks tomorrow.'

'Very good,' Mr Daven murmured as he began to fill in the forms. He asked them questions when needed, although they were more directed at Cormac as he knew most of Victoria's details already.

'And will you take on the name of Blake?' Mr Daven asked, pausing at another box. After a few moments of silence, both men turned to Victoria whose face had gone completely blank, but not in the same way it had when she'd stepped off the lift.

Cormac suspected in all her planning, she hadn't thought of such a question. He certainly didn't expect her to. After all it was *she* who was a member of the royal house, *she* who was the Lady Snape—it was kind of in her title. Her father had been Avalone's richest man outside of the Royal Family and there was no way she would-

'Yes.' She nodded her head to confirm it. 'I will be Lady Victoria Georgina Blake.'

'Very well.' The solicitor ticked another box, continuing through his legal list while the thought sank into Cormac's brain.

In seven weeks, he'd have a wife. He'd be a married man. Mr and Mrs Cormac Blake.

No, Mr and *Lady* Cormac Blake.

'I have to say,' Mr Daven said as he signed the documents in a couple of places before he turned them around and presented them to Victoria. 'I know King Richard is far-reaching, but even I will be impressed if he can organise a royal wedding in just seven weeks.'

'It's already mostly done,' Victoria said as she signed where the old man indicated after briefly checking through the document. 'The cathedral's been booked since the day after we finished mourning.'

'Without an official announcement?' Cormac found himself asking. He might not be the most on-the-ball person when it came to pop culture, but even he knew that you needed an official and legal notice of intention to marry before you could book a wedding venue. Victoria lifted her eyes to meet his.

'Okay, so it's more like *pencilled in*, but as the bishop said, if I married on that date or not, the cathedral is at my disposal that Saturday. And if he's given it to someone else, he'll have the King to deal with.' She slid the documents over to Cormac with a smirk. Clearly, she was happy to have the royal connection in this instance.

'How much of this have you planned?' Cormac asked, his mind blown as he took the proffered pen. Victoria sighed, resting her head in her hand as she leaned on the table and looked at him.

'Pretty much everything is on reserve. Nothing has been

paid for though. I wasn't able to give any deposits either, so I only have verbal promises.'

'What idiot would cancel on the first royal wedding in thirty years?' Mr Daven piped up as he reached over the desk and pointed at a line on the announcement form next to where Victoria had squiggled her signature, a loopy *Lady Victoria G Snape*. 'Sign here, Mr Blake.'

Cormac glanced down at the document. He'd never seen one before, never really been involved in a wedding outside of attending as a mere guest. He'd never been the best man, or even had the chance of playing the role of an usher. He'd been left behind by his friends after they'd gone on to university or headed into successful career paths while he'd been trying to juggle parental and financial responsibilities and failing miserably at both.

He glanced up at Victoria, his pen hovering over the line.

'Can I ask for one more thing?'

Victoria blinked, a little surprised, but nodded.

'I'd like to go to University. Or do an apprenticeship. Something that will teach me about money and investments and things like that.' A smile ticked up the corner of her mouth. She held Cormac's gaze, and he saw a flicker of self-satisfaction within her caramel eyes.

'Did you get that, Mr Daven?'

'Yes,' the solicitor said with a long-suffering sigh. 'Will you be looking at attending right away?' Cormac shook his head. 'Very well, just keep me appraised of your intentions.'

Cormac couldn't stop the wide grin that broke across his face at Mr Daven's words and signed the papers. He was going to go to University. He was going to get a degree. He'd be able to understand where he'd gone wrong with his finances, how he'd been ripped off, and perhaps, in the future, he'd be able to help those who were in the same situation.

'And the last one there.'

But first he had to become a husband.

He signed the final line.

∼

Victoria and Cormac left *Cartwright, Daven, Mercer, and Associates*, quite quickly after signing the official announcement forms, intending to return next week to finalise the agreement between them before their intention to marry was published in the Avon Guardian. As soon as it appeared, they'd *officially* be able to begin planning the wedding. Victoria had always thought she'd leave such an occasion walking on cloud nine, a skip in her step as she held hands with her beloved, putting their heads together to whisper how excited they were at their upcoming nuptials. While she didn't feel like she had a ten-pound weight around her neck, she didn't feel the elation she'd always dreamt she would.

Cormac had been noticeably quiet afterwards and continued to be so as he stared out of the window, lost in what looked like deep thoughts. Victoria left him to them. He had a lot to go over, a lot to come to terms with, and things to consider as new opportunities were now open to him and his brother.

Meanwhile, she took the chance to quietly tap away on her phone, checking and rechecking she had access to her accounts and cards again. It was such a relief after a difficult few months, borrowing money from her sisters here and there when she didn't want to use the royal purse. She tapped out a few messages, sent a couple of emails, and added several appointments to her calendar for Kirstie to arrange. After authorising some quick transfers to her sisters to repay each of them, she switched off her phone again to avoid the panicked calls she knew she'd get from her secretary if she didn't.

'I was wondering,' Victoria broke the silence as they neared Cormac's block of flats. 'If perhaps you and James would like to join me for lunch?'

'I don't know if—'

'It would be good for people to see us in public a couple of time before the announcement goes out on Friday.' It was only a week away, but if they were at least *seen* together there would be less speculation. There was always going to be *some*. The media were going to be desperate to know what had happened for her to go from sudden dating spree to engaged in the blink of an eye. But she knew Kirstie would help her spin it as they'd been dating quietly, that she knew her grandfather wouldn't approve of someone as *common*—she hated that word—as Cormac, so had kept the relationship secret.

Their story would be that Cormac eventually decided enough was enough; it was either him forever or never. She'd initially panicked and broken it off just before her father died, and the stream of men afterwards were rebounds and grief. It was only after the attack that she realised she'd been a fool and knew she could never be without Cormac. She'd gone to him, begged him to still love her—of course, he'd say something sappy like he'd never stopped—and accepted his proposal if he still wanted to marry her.

He would insist on a whirlwind engagement to ensure she never had to be without him and so he knew she was always safe.

She'd go over the premise with Cormac tomorrow, ensure that he understood why they needed such a backstory. They'd have to make it convincing, because this was not only what she was going to tell the King, but what the world would be fed. If they couldn't convince her grandfather of the truth, they'd never convince the public.

'Okay,' Cormac said. He hesitated for a moment before adding, 'But nowhere too fancy.'

'Of course.'

'I just... Let's start slow with introducing us into *that* life, yeah?'

Victoria's lips pouted as she tried to figure out how best to answer that comment.

'You do understand that's not possible, Cormac? We'll be married in seven weeks. You must meet my family very quickly. The King is probably going to demand a meeting as soon as the news reaches him.' Victoria noted the colour drained from his face. She reached out and gently took his hand in hers. Her own looked so tiny and dainty around his.

'Cormac, you're going to have to learn a lot of things in very quick succession. I know you're far from stupid,' she added quickly when he made to speak. 'But you're literally going to be bombarded with protocols and rules, names of a lot of people and significant facts about them. These are things you're going to have to know off the top of your head, with no notes to check through beforehand.'

He glanced down at their hands when she squeezed his gently. 'It's not going to be easy,' she confessed. 'But I'll help you as much as I can, whenever I can, I promise.'

'Thank you,' he whispered.

Victoria sighed as she sat back but didn't let go of his fingers. She pulled the corner of her lower lip into her mouth as she considered her fiancé. She wondered if he was reliving the last time his life had changed so much in one day. The day his parents died and he became James' only family.

'How about you pick where we go?' She smiled at him as he lifted his gaze to hers. 'You could pick somewhere you've been wanting to go to. *Or* somewhere James keeps pestering to try?' He huffed a laugh at that, one side of his mouth lifting into a lopsided smile she wanted to kiss.

'Kid's got a hearty appetite and *loves* meat.' He shook his head as his smiled widened. A little spark lit his eyes, and Victoria knew he had somewhere in mind. 'There's a place that you can go to that's *all you can eat,* but it's all meat,' he continued. 'Steaks, ribs, wings, pulled pork, burgers, sausages… They give you a card and you put it on green and they just bring you over selections of meat to take from their trolley. When you're full or need to pause, you turn it over to red.'

Victoria felt a little sick at the thought of such a place, and it must have shown on her face as he quickly dropped his smile and said, 'It's probably not the right sort of place really, is it?'

No, it really wasn't, but this was something he wanted, and she was already taking so much from him. Plus, their story was that their different lives had caused some conflict between them. Maybe they could say that she had kept expecting *him* to rise and meet her at her level, when really, she had to put in the effort and meet him halfway.

'Okay.' She nodded. 'Let's get James and go there. If you know the address, I'll get Toby to find it while you grab your brother.'

'Thank you!' He leaned over and pressed a kiss to her cheek. Her breath hitched at the contact, and she turned to him as he pulled back. He paused in his retreat, staring down at her, his lips just a breath away from her own. Her heart thundered in her chest. She could just lean forward, just tilt her head ever so slightly and press her lips to his and finally taste the man she was dying to sample.

He licked his lips as he stared back, his own eyes dropping to take in her mouth as she mirrored him.

'Can… Can I kiss you?' He breathed the words more than spoke them, and Victoria swore she could hear his racing heart.

She didn't answer. Instead, she closed the gap between them and pressed her mouth to his. The merest brush of her lips, a caress, a whisper of a kiss, a promise of so much more.

She gently pushed him back towards his side of the car.

His breathing was ragged, his chest rising and falling as his eyes drank her in, reclining in her seat, the skirt of her dress up again just enough for that tease of lace, her small chest straining against her clothes as she tried to calm her own breathing.

'Go get your brother,' she told him, her voice low and husky.

'Right, yeah,' he said, but still didn't move. 'Victoria…' He made to lean towards her again, and Victoria gasped, waiting for the crush of his lips on hers, for him to take what his eyes told her he wanted. This time, she'd allow it, she'd embrace it, welcome it-

Clunk.

The door handle of the car was depressed, and a sliver of daylight pierced their silent sanctuary. Cormac jumped, turning so quickly in his seat that Victoria winced at the motion.

'Sir, ma'am,' Toby said, peering inside when neither of them immediately climbed out.

'Go get James,' she repeated. Cormac glanced back at her one more time and she shifted her legs slightly, allowing her skirt to inch up a little higher. He groaned before stepping out of the car and jogging up the pavement to the staircase.

'Toby, we're going for lunch,' she told the driver before he could close the door. 'Mr Blake will give you the name of the restaurant upon his return.'

'Very good, ma'am.'

The moment he closed the door, Victoria slid down in her seat with a frustrated wail and waited for the return of her soon-to-be lover.

CHAPTER TEN

'Oh, here he is!' Geri's distinctive voice called down the corridor from the offices to the top of the stairs as Cormac reached their peak. 'His royal commander, prince and saviour of damsels in distress everywhere.'

'Piss off, Geri,' he shouted back before ducking into the break room. His eye caught the couch where he'd settled Victoria when he'd rescued her, and vividly recalled how he'd wondered what her lips would feel like against his. Their kiss yesterday had been the lightest, chastest kiss he'd ever got from a woman he wasn't related to, but it had only stoked the burning desire he already held for her. He'd had to ensure she hadn't kissed him again later when she'd dropped the Blake duo back home after their lunch, unsure he could trust himself to keep it PG-rated in front of James.

'So, did she give you a knighthood? Do I need to prostrate myself at your feet to gain favour with you?' Geri stood in the doorway; her pierced brow was raised in question as she watched him put his things into his locker.

'Yeah, I'm now Sir Cormac, lord of I'll-kick-your-arse-into-next-week-if-you-don't-do-one.'

'Alright, duchess, don't get your knickers in a twist!' She held up her hands as she spoke, in an *I surrender* gesture.

Wait! his brain screamed. She hadn't teased him about the whole rescue in days, not since O'Malley had pulled him up and he'd been marched off the premises that night. When he'd turned up the next day, he could see she was itching to talk about it, but he'd told her he didn't want to and they'd left it at that.

'How'd you know I'd seen Victoria again?' he asked, feigning nonchalance as he closed his cubby and locked it.

'Ooh, so it's *Victoria* now, is it? I supposed when she's pressing kisses to your cheek, you get to be on first-name basis.' Cormac froze.

'Say what?' he said quietly, turning only his head towards his friend. Victoria *had* kissed his cheek yesterday. She'd done it as they were leaving the restaurant when he'd stood up and wrapped her shawl around her shoulders. She'd leaned up and pecked his cheek, which was proceeded by a blush on his side and James making gagging sounds.

'Your pictures are all over the media!' she said. 'Please don't tell me- Fuck's sake, Cormac you really need to step into the twenty-first century and get a smartphone!' She pulled her own sleek device from her pocket and unlocked it with a swipe of her finger before she began tapping away as she walked to him.

'Here!' she said, thrusting it in his face. He stared at it, completely agog, as he recognised himself standing in the restaurant. Victoria's hands lay over his while they rested on her shoulders, as she reached up and kissed his cheek.

When he saw the *1 of 12* pictures in the top right-hand corner of the image, he grabbed the phone from Geri's fingers and swiped left.

There were pictures of the three of them reading their menus, Cormac helping James up onto a booster seat, his little legs swinging high above the ground as he sucked on his milkshake. The three of them laughing as the first cart was wheeled to them and Victoria shooed them away instead, telling them to bring a tomahawk steak to the table —the biggest they had! James had nearly fallen out of his chair when he'd spied it, and Cormac had considered asking for a mop with the drool the kid produced as it was put in front of the trio.

Then there were more pictures of them leaving, and suddenly the kiss wasn't the most telling of all the pictures. After wrapping her up and receiving his peck, he'd guided her through the throng of people, his hand on the small of her back, keeping her close and safe, as James walked in front of them.

He squinted down at one of the pictures as they left, before Geri sighed and leaned in, using her fingers to make the picture bigger. James was holding Victoria's hand! Cormac was stunned by the move. His little brother was so particular about who he allowed into his personal space, often hiding behind Cormac's leg as he peered at people.

He dropped the phone from his scrutiny and stared into space, trying to fathom what had made his brother take someone else's hand.

'I can't believe you took her to *The Meat Hut*, Cormac,' Geri said as she took her phone away from him and continued to flick through the pictures. 'I thought you'd have a bit more class than that! She's a *real* lady after all. They go to fancy places, like...'

Cormac sank down to the couch. Was this to be his life? Would he and James be hounded by the press? Would the two be harassed whenever they went out? Would people be clamouring for pictures of them just doing the most mundane things? That had been day one; how bad would it get by day ten? Or twenty? What about day one thousand, eight hundred and sixty-two when the five years of marriage ended? He tried not to consider what might happen if they didn't have to end it…

He'd grown up thinking marriage was forever, not a means for inheritance, titles, or payments. So, he wasn't sure if, when the time came to walk away, he'd be able to—especially if there was a child involved.

But he couldn't subject James to this, to random people thinking it was fine for them to snap pictures of him whenever they liked.

'Cormac, are you okay?' Geri asked, interrupting his thoughts as she sat beside him. 'You've gone a little pale.'

'They're going to pester us, aren't they?' he said quietly, still staring into nothing. 'They'll snap us whenever and wherever…'

'Who? People? The press? Nah, they'll get bored in a day or two when she's off with the next guy-'

Cormac snorted. Of course, that's what they *would* think. Right now, he was just the new face in a long line of faces and when they couldn't get anything on him—after all, if the head of the Royal Guard couldn't get anything some random reporter wasn't going to be able to—they'd start talking about who would be next on her radar… Until they saw them together again, then it would *really* blow up.

His stomach rolled as he realised that would come on Friday when their marriage announcement would be printed. And once that was published, as long as no one came forward by their set date to contest their nuptials, they were legally married. There wasn't actually a legal requirement for a service—religious or civil—but who didn't want a celebration of their love?

Cormac would definitely have preferred *not* to have the sort of celebration they were going to have to endure. A small family event would have been his preference, not TV cameras streaming it live around the world.

'Cormac?' Geri's hand gently squeezed his shoulder and tried to turn him slightly to look at her. 'Is there something the matter?' He sighed softly as he glanced at the only person he was probably able to call a friend. Her heavily made-up eyes—she had her purple contacts in today—searched his. He wished he could tell her everything, that he could just get it all off his chest. Everything had just gone completely batshit crazy over the last couple of days, and he wished he had someone outside of his head to talk to. Maybe she'd be able to walk him through everything, make him see for certain that he'd done the right thing. That he definitely *shouldn't* tell O'Malley what Victoria had offered; it wasn't as if he'd need this job in a few days…

Cormac rubbed his hands over his face as he groaned, shaking his head. He couldn't tell her anything. He'd made a promise and wouldn't break it. No matter how much it was eating him up.

'I'm fine, Smurf. Just tired.'

'They have blue *skin*,' she told him with a light slap to the back of his head. 'You really should know this with a baby brother.'

'He doesn't seem to watch cartoons anymore, prefers to be blowing heads off zombies.'

'You've got to stop letting him play those games, Cormac. He's going to lose all that brain power.'

'Kid's got plenty to spare.' She nodded her agreement before patting his shoulder.

'Well, we gotta get you undressed and oiled up. Magda will be in the audience tonight; she's watching everyone's solos, so be prepared.'

Cormac groaned, rolling his head back across his shoulders. Well, at least he didn't have to do this for much longer. He was ready to speak to O'Malley on Friday as soon as the announcement appeared, then he'd cut all ties and hand in his immediate notice.

'Yeah, alright,' he said, as he gathered his t-shirt before

pulling it over his head. 'Grab the oil for me, Ger, and let's get this show on the road.'

'The things I do for this job,' she said with a smirk as she grabbed the baby oil from the table. Cormac rolled his eyes as he began to unbuckle his jeans.

∼

Cormac eased his bright yellow Beetle to a stop and wrenched the handbrake up to ensure it didn't try and roll away again. Twice this week, he'd found it a few feet from where he'd originally parked it. He'd tried complaining to the garage that had supposedly fixed it, but the bastards refused to even acknowledge him.

Maybe he'd ask Victoria to borrow one of her fancy cars and go visit them again. Then when they started to kiss his arse to get their hands on such a luxury vehicle—and the money that came with it—he'd give them the fingers and have Toby drive them away.

He chuckled at the thought, the image painted perfectly in his mind as he grabbed his bag and unfolded himself from his car, locking the door behind him. He tucked his keys into his pocket, threw his bag over his shoulder and began to jog across the car park towards the darkened stairwell.

He paused in his step, frowning at the pillar of darkness he trudged up in the early hours of every morning. His eyes followed the concrete block upwards and across the landings that sheltered the doorways of the flats. Some were in darkness, and the ones that had lights were only lit sporadically, some flickering in their dingy units, but there were some landings in complete darkness. Usually, his own landing had a light on right outside his door, which was probably why he'd never really noticed the level of deprivation before, but right now it was blown out.

He glanced around the courtyard; there was a lack of

green anywhere save the bins that overflowed with rubbish, spilling onto the floor as if it had vomited over the concrete slabs that provided a poor play area for the children. He knew he lived in a dump but had always considered himself lucky to just have a home, to not complain or raise his head. Why the hell was he paying so much to live in such a state? Surely, they should be paying *him* to even take on such a dive.

He wondered what Victoria's thoughts had been when she'd first arrived and why she didn't just turn and flee at the sight of his hovel. He shook his head, wondering why she'd still offered him such a deal after seeing all this, and was about to continue on his way, when the sound of a slowly rolling car caught his attention.

His first thought was of his Beetle. He turned to see the car exactly where it was supposed to be, before snapping his head in the other direction as the sound continued.

A long, dark car slowly pulled its way up the street. Cormac's stomach dropped at the realisation the car's lights were off; they didn't want people to see them coming... And he had a feeling he knew exactly who it was that was coming. For him.

He stepped up onto the kerb and turned to face the car as it slowed to a stop beside him. The back window lowered, the whirr of its electric motor loud in the darkness of night, but it didn't reveal anyone inside. Cormac moved his head to try and see who was in there, his brow raising as the bright red burn of embers appeared, floating in the middle of the black abyss.

'To what do I owe the pleasure, Mr O'Malley?' he asked without preamble.

'Get in,' the other man said. The door on the other side of the car opened and one of his enormous bodyguards climbed out. Cormac sighed before trudging around the car and climbing into the dark compartment. The door closed immediately behind him, plunging him into darkness, the faint glow at the end of O'Malley's cigar their only light.

'You were supposed to call me,' O'Malley said. The dim light moved upwards before burning brightly as O'Malley puffed on the stogie. 'I saw the images this morning, and I waited by the phone all day for your call. Do you think I like feeling like a bitch in heat waiting for her man to call for a fuck?'

Cormac was glad for the darkness so O'Malley couldn't see his face twisting into disgust at the picture the other man painted. Who the hell spoke like that?

'I thought you'd be at the club this evening,' he said, the lie coming so easily. 'I planned to tell you there.'

O'Malley made a humming noise that Cormac knew meant he didn't believe him, but wouldn't call him on it. The little light lifted and burned brightly again a second later, and Cormac leaned back towards the door as the thick cloud of smoke filled the air again.

'And what did you plan on telling me? What did the little lady offer?'

'She thanked me, took me and my little brother for lunch —she actually allowed *him* to choose-'

O'Malley laughed, a dry, hacking laugh at that titbit.

'It *was* a bit surprising to see a lady of such standing in the middle of *The Meat Hut*. Now I understand. But what did she *offer* you?'

Cormac opened his mouth to speak and then closed it again, considering O'Malley's words.

'She didn't *offer* me anything,' he said, truthfully. 'She *thanked* me, paid for lunch and said if there was anything she could give me to help my situation, she'd be more than happy to help.'

The light of the cigar end lit up again before the other man spoke.

'Okay, kid, if that's how you want to play it.' The door to

the car opened and Cormac didn't hesitate in leaving the car. The bodyguard who had given up his seat a few moments ago faced him.

'We'll be in touch,' the goon told him.

'Why?' Cormac frowned.

'Because we know you're lying.'

'I'm done,' Cormac said, firmly. 'I did *exactly* what he said.'

'No, kid, you didn't, and that's going to come back on you *and* your little brother.

Cormac didn't need to think, he got right up in tall guy's face and snarled, 'She didn't *offer* anything save for a hot meal and a ride in a fancy car. So, whatever you *think* you know, you can forget. But you *will* understand that I. Am. Done.' He shoved the guy away from him, causing him to stumble backwards, losing his footing and falling to the hard-tarmacked road. Cormac sneered down at the goon as he hoisted his bag up further on his shoulder.

'You know what?' He turned and banged on the roof of the car. 'You can shove your job. I don't need it. Hear that, O'Malley. I don't need you, your money, or any favours. I am done. *Done!*'

'Hey, keep it down!' someone shouted from out a window high above them.

The goon stood up quickly and pushed Cormac out of the way as he scrambled inside the car. Cormac continued to shout, really making sure he made a spectacle of the situation.

'And if you threaten my brother again, I'll make sure it's the *last* thing you do! Now go on!' He really raised his voice. 'Get out of here! We don't need the likes of you in this place, threatening little kids, you perverts!'

'He's threatening kids?' another voice shouted down.

'Yeah!' Cormac called back.

'I'm calling the police!' a third voice bellowed down. 'I got the plates! I've got pictures on my phone!'

The door slammed behind the hired thug, and the car burst to life, squealing away from Cormac and out of the courtyard.

'Oi! I've got kids sleeping up here!' screeched a woman. 'Keep it down the lot of you!'

Cormac raced up the stairs to his flat and ran along the corridor to his door as his unknown neighbours began to bicker between themselves. Lights flickered on throughout the buildings as more people were disturbed by the shouting and screaming of the arguments.

'You okay?' Mrs Battersea asked as she came hurrying from the living room as fast as she could, as he all but fell into the flat's hallway.

'Where's James?' he asked, breathlessly, clinging onto the door for dear life as his chest rose and fell as he caught his breath. The old woman looked at him as if he'd gone mad, but every instinct in him screamed he needed to see James, to hold his little body in his arms and know he was okay.

'He's in bed, of course.' He marched to the door. 'Don't you go waking up that lad!' she scolded, putting a hand on his chest and pushing him back before he charged inside.

'He's sleeping, and there's no reason for you to wake him. Understand?' She looked up at him with a challenge in her eyes. She was right, he was acting like a hothead.

She'd have told him if something had happened; she'd have called the club immediately and left him a message.

He took a deep breath to calm his racing heart and quell the rising panic in him before he peeked his head through the gap between the door and the wall.

James lay in the bed, his head twisted on his pillow, his body contorted in a way that only kids could find comfortable enough to sleep in. His soft snores were music to Cormac's ears, and he found himself smiling as he took in the whole picture.

Cormac bit his lip as he watched the gentle rise and fall of

James' chest; James was safe, warm, and hopefully dreaming of the better life they were about to embark on.

But he wasn't safe. Neither of them were when O'Malley knew where they lived and was openly threatening them.

He closed his eyes, fighting against the well of anger that surged up at O'Malley, Mrs Battersea, James, his parents and even himself—*especially* himself—for them being in such a situation. If James hadn't been born or if his parents hadn't died, if the con artist hadn't scammed him out of his savings, if O'Malley hadn't offered him the deal or Mrs Battersea hadn't talked him into going back to the dick…

If he had stood by his own decision to say *no* to O'Malley and not be talked into making bad choices *again*…

'Cormac?' Mrs Battersea reached out to touch his arm gently, but he shook her hand away.

He was utterly useless, everything he did turned to shit, and Cormac was done making bad decisions. Right now, he had to listen to his heart because his head clearly didn't know what it was doing.

'Can you watch him a few minutes more?' he asked without looking at the older woman.

'Of course,' she said quietly, as if suddenly unsure of him.

He ran back out of the flat and down the stairs to the payphone he'd stopped at just a few nights ago when he'd monumentally fucked up. He raced to the phone, skidding to a stop, both hands hitting the metal behind the phone to stop himself from ploughing straight into the thing. He paused to catch his breath before he reached out for the receiver where his hand hesitated.

He couldn't tell Victoria what he'd done. She'd tell him where to go—no matter how desperate she was for a husband. And if she didn't marry him, he was stuck here, with no job again. He'd be right back where he'd been three nights ago, save for the giant target he now had on his back for telling O'Malley to go fuck himself.

'Shit,' he cursed as he leaned his head back and stared up at the sky as if it could give him all the answers.

He couldn't tell her, *but* he couldn't stay here for long. It wasn't safe anymore.

He picked up the receiver and dropped what few coins he had into the phone before searching through his wallet for the piece of paper with her number.

The line rang two, three, four times… He was about to hang up when a sleepy voice answered.

'Hello,' Victoria said groggily, her voice husky with sleep. Cormac felt an overwhelming rush of conflicting emotions run over him.

'Victoria? It's Cormac,' he said, holding the receiver close and lowering his voice in case anyone was listening. He had no idea if O'Malley had left someone behind. Shit, he should have thought of *that* before.

'Cormac?' She suddenly sounded a lot more awake. 'Is everything okay?'

He took a deep breath to prepare himself for the web of deceit he was going to have to spin.

'No, not really. I… er…'

'Cormac, what is it? Is it James?'

'No, well, yes, well, it affects him.' He sighed deeply. 'The eviction, the landlord left a message for me when I'd got home, it's still proceeding. Apparently, he doesn't trust me to maintain the payments going forward.'

'He can do that?' she asked.

'Yes,' he croaked, unsure if it was true or not. 'I don't… I need somewhere to stay. I don't know if you can help at all?'

'Of course.' He heard her scrambling about, the bedsheets ruffling and shifting, and he wondered briefly what she was wearing before he shook the thought off. He had more important things to be thinking of.

'When do you need to be out by?'

'As soon as possible. Today if I can.'

'That soon?' she sounded surprised and confused. 'I mean'—Cormac bet she was cursing herself for not knowing these kind of things—'not a problem, I'm sure I can move things up, or find a replacement if I can't. Is a hotel okay until we find a place together? We can put your things in storage, and I can have a removal van there this afternoon.'

'Everything we need can fit into my car; the rest can go to the dump.' She went so quiet, Cormac thought she'd disconnected the call.

'I'll have a car come and fetch you. Can you be ready by midday?'

'Princess, I can be ready by 8am.'

'I'm afraid that I'd need until at least noon.' Cormac bit his lip and glanced at the watch on his wrist. It was two-thirty now; could he wait almost ten hours? Mind, once he was packed, James wouldn't take too long. They could go for breakfast and make a morning of it, ensuring they were back in time.

'Okay, midday.'

'Hmm... Actually, I'll have the men there before ten-thirty. I'll send a car for you.' She sounded far more alert now, and he imagined she was already on that tablet of hers, making things happen.

'I have a car.'

'I'm having that taken away; it looked like a death trap—unless there's sentimentality behind it?' She suddenly sounded unsure. She was probably thinking it may have been his parents' or even a gift from them at one point. He wanted to scoff at the thought.

'Nah, trust me, that thing is nothing but a headache.'

'Then I'll have it sorted along with the stuff from the flat.' And Cormac didn't doubt her. 'I'll see you later, Cormac.'

'Yeah, see you then, princess.'

'I'm not a princess, Cormac,' she reminded him before she hung up.

Cormac gently put the receiver back in its cradle before turning and, with slouching shoulders, slowly made his way back to the flat. If she wasn't a princess, she must be a fairy godmother, he decided as he mentally began sorting through what he was going to take with him and what they were leaving behind. Again.

TO BE CONTINUED

TAKING HIM - SAMPLE
THE ROYALS OF AVALON'S - INHERITANCE: VICTORIA PART 2

Available to buy NOW

'C'mon, James!' Cormac shouted back into the flat as he jiggled the box he was holding to try and get a better grip. They didn't have much to take, but the few personal items they did have, he wanted to ensure they got to wherever they were going in one piece.

James was still pouting over the fact they had to move again, although Cormac failed to see exactly *why* his little brother was dawdling—*anywhere* had to be better than here. Cormac was not going to miss the tepid showers—even when he turned the temperature up to max. Or the hob he had to keep checking was off because he'd occasionally smell gas as he walked by. Or having to sleep on a sofa bed far too small for his large frame.

'I'm here,' James said with a tone Cormac had believed he wouldn't hear until his brother hit at least thirteen, but had prayed it would be never.

'Drop the attitude,' Cormac told him, shifting the weight of the heavy box of the few family mementos they had from one arm to the other. 'I don't know why you're moping so much about this. Think you'd be grateful to get a proper bedroom, more than likely with your own flat panel TV and all the consoles you'd ever want.'

James merely shrugged in response, pulling his little suitcase over the threshold, and heading towards the stairs. Cormac rolled his eyes and hoped his brother didn't trip over his own lip with how much it was sticking out.

'And that should just be those cases left then,' Cormac told the two guys standing in the hallway. He'd told Victoria he didn't need a whole van, but she'd sent one anyway, even if it was on the smaller side. Their meagre possessions—a couple of suitcases, boxes of James' toys and books, his own smaller collection of fiction and textbooks, a box of a few personal bits, and the box in his arms filled with the only pictures and a couple of keepsakes he had left from his parents—looked rather sad and pathetic in the long-wheel-based Transit van.

'We'll drop you off at the hotel,' one of the removal men told him. 'Get everything up there and then come back here for the rest. You said *everything* left to a disposal site? Are you sure you don't want to donate some of it?'

Cormac shook his head. 'I got almost everything *from* charity stores years ago—if you're able to get them downstairs in one piece, I'll be amazed,' he confessed. The men grabbed the bags and hauled them up on their shoulders in a way that said they'd done this hundreds of times before. He let the two men go before him, so he could both lock up and not hold them up on the stairwell as he carefully made his way down with his box of treasures.

James sat on the kerb a few feet from the back of the van, his elbows rested on his knobbly knees and his hands cupping his face. He was kept company by his little suitcase carefully placed next to him. The picture was so pitiful it hurt.

Cormac sighed, shifting the box to hold it in one hand as he reached down and ruffled James' hair, making a mental note it needed a cut again.

'C'mon, buddy. Chin up. Whatever we're going to *is* going to be better than here. You do believe that, don't you?'

'Yeah,' James said glumly, making Cormac even more puzzled. But, with a very weary sigh for a six-year-old, James pushed himself to his feet and pulled his little case along the few feet to the back of the van where one of the removal men waited patiently for the brothers. Reluctantly, Cormac handed the guy his box and watched as the man carefully put it into another, foam-lined, container. Cormac raised his brow.

'If we'd had time, sir, we'd have packed everything for you in these.' Cormac had to admit they did look a lot more secure than the cardboard ones he'd used.

'Is that to go in too, young sir?' the man crouched down and asked James, nodding towards his little case.

'I suppose,' he said quietly with a little shrug.

Cormac moved to the front of the van, looking for where Toby would be parked. But he couldn't see a Rolls Royce anywhere. Instead, he saw a sleek black car parked a few cars down on the opposite side of the road. Just as he spied the luxury sedan, it pulled out of its spot and made its way towards them.

As the Bentley Mulsanne pulled up, Cormac resisted the urge to open the door himself and climb inside, remembering how Victoria always waited for the driver. It seemed pointless when he had to wait and could easily just open the door himself, but if he was going to live in Victoria's world, he had to begin to follow her rules—even if they were stupid.

'Whoa,' James said, taking in the shiny black car.

The younger Blake seemed more impressed with this one

than the one they'd been in just two days ago. 'Can I sit in the front?'

'Afraid not,' Cormac said as the driver opened the rear door and ushered the pair inside.

It was a long journey for a six-year-old, even in a car as amazing as this one. After playing with every button he could reach, moving every knob and lever, flicking through the TV channels on the small screen in front of him, the questions Cormac always dreaded started. And without knowing where they were going, he couldn't answer James' incessant *are we there yet?* And *how long now?*

'Dude, I *don't know*,' he said after the twelfth time. 'We'll be there when we get there.' Cormac saw the driver glancing his way in the rear-view mirror and Cormac knew he wasn't supposed to speak unless spoken to first. 'Hey, bud, sorry I didn't catch your name.'

'William, sir,' the driver said, his eyes quickly flickering to Cormac before refocusing on the road.

'Nice to meet you, Will, could you tell us where we're going?'

'Sorry, sir, but I'm afraid that Lady Snape requested I not reveal that information.'

Cormac snorted. *Requested*. She had probably demanded it. He still wasn't too sure which version of the woman he'd met was the real one, but he had to admit that he was kind of looking forward to finding out. Particularly if the real Victoria was the one he'd kissed in the back of the car.

The car twisted and turned its way through the capital's streets, hampered by the ever-present traffic cities seemed to be forever caught up in. But as the car turned down Main Street, Cormac's heart began to speed up, his breath caught in his throat. There was only one hotel on this street and there was no *way* they could be staying there. From his earlier days of taxiing through the city, he knew the money that lined the pockets of the people who stayed there. It was where Heads of State were housed when they visited. There was no way he could afford even the most basic of rooms at the Denyer Hotel.

But then he wasn't paying for it, and Victoria *was* a member of the Royal Family. He really needed to get his head around this whole thing and quickly.

The car slowed and pulled into the curved driveway of the most expensive, most glamorous hotel in all Avalone. The Denyer hotel was known throughout the world as the height of luxury, and anyone who was anyone wanted to secure rooms—even a basic one—when they had the option, just to be able to say they were staying at such an establishment. His mouth fell open at the idea that he and James would be staying at such a place. Never in his wildest dreams would he have ever thought of stepping foot through the doors of such an establishment.

When he'd been a bellboy at a lower-end hotel—one he still couldn't afford to stay in—a few streets over, he and others from other hotels would hang around on lunch breaks, talking about who they'd seen that day, what type of tips they'd had, and so on, but the bellhops from the Denyer had never graced their breaks. They may have held the same job as them, but their bellboys—the cleaners too!—were all graduates, working their way up in the hotelier industry, desperate to be spotted by Niles Denyer one day.

'Look at those men in the weird hats,' James said pressing his nose against the window to get a better look at the impeccably dressed doormen.

'I think you might have the wrong place,' Cormac said to the driver just before they stopped.

'No, sir.'

One of the doormen opened the car door and James almost tumbled out at the unexpected action. Without even glancing back at his older brother, James jumped from the car and stood on the pavement, head craned back to stare up at what seemed an impossibly tall building for a six-year-old.

'Whoa,' he breathed. 'Corrie, look.' He pointed up at the flags that billowed majestically with the breeze coming in from the ocean, high above the entrance.

'Yeah,' Cormac said distractedly, giving them a cursory glance as he peered around for the van with their belongings which should have been following them.

'They've gone to the delivery entrance,' William told Cormac as he came around the car, seemingly knowing Cormac's thoughts. He supposed they were probably paid for such mind-reading skills. 'They'll use the service lift to take your possessions up. Cormac's heart leapt into his mouth at the idea of his box of treasures being lost or dropped.

'Don't worry, sir, the men were personally chosen by Lady Victoria. Here'—the driver handed Cormac a small silver card—'show this to the lift attendant and they'll take you directly up.'

'I don't need to check in?' The other man shook his head.

'All taken care of, sir. I wish you well.'

Cormac lifted his hand in a half-hearted wave, his mind whirling with questions and self-doubts and the realisation he was *well* out of his depth.

'Corrie, is this where we're staying?'

'I guess so,' he said, his own head tilting back as he too became hypnotised by the dancing flags as he tried to get his head around the fact.

'This is so... *cool!*' James exclaimed. 'Can we go in? Can we?' His brother grabbed the hem of his t-shirt and tugged on it, fruitlessly trying to make his brother move. Cormac looked down at the kid, noting that his eyes were now bright with anticipation and wonder, eager to see what else awaited him. The grin that split wide across his face was a far cry from the pout that had graced his lips earlier, and he bounced on the balls of his feet, suddenly desperate to move and needing to do it quickly.

Cormac nodded and grabbed James' shoulder as he tried to race off into the grand building. He was fairly sure people who stayed here didn't run through throngs of people, darting around them as if they were an obstacle course.

'Hold my hand, bud.'

'Aww, Corrie-'

'No. No arguing on this. This isn't a place to run about in, and I don't want you getting lost.' He glanced down at the key card in his hand again; it seemed to shimmer in the morning sun. This was his way into something bigger and better for both James and himself, and if he was going to survive this for as long as he'd need to, he was going to have to throw himself into everything Victoria asked him to.

He squared his shoulders, fixed the neck on his t-shirt from where James had pulled it out of shape with his pleading, and stepped forward, reminding himself that he belonged here.

He flashed the doorman a smile and nodded to the older gentleman as the man held the large gold and glass door open for him.

'Good day, sir,' the man said. Cormac nodded his head at the guy.

He kept tight hold of James as they strode through the lobby. A few members of staff raised their eyebrows at him, dressed in a plain white t-shirt and faded jeans—clearly not designer—but he kept his head up high.

He'd almost reached the bank of lifts when a large gentleman, dressed in the colours of the hotel, stepped in front of him, stopping the duo in their tracks. James stepped closer to his brother and Cormac automatically pulled him against his side.

'Excuse me, sir.' The man's voice was deep, shaking the

very air around them, making Cormac's hair stand on end. 'Only guests are permitted to the rooms.'

Cormac cursed himself as he felt his brows raising high, and his cheeks heating up. People walking by and getting into the lifts he'd been heading towards were starting to pay attention to them, their eyes filled with judgement, finding him wanting despite having no clue who he was or any connections he might have. Part of him wanted to tell them all he was about to marry into royalty, that they'd soon be lining up to catch a glimpse of him at the first royal wedding in over a quarter of a century, but he quickly stamped that part of himself down. The announcement wouldn't go out until Friday and if it got out before Victoria was ready for it, he'd ruin all her plans.

He quickly schooled his face into one of utter contempt, mirroring those around him. He kept his eyes on the man—probably security—as he brought the silver card up level with his face.

'I *am* a guest.'

The human barricade glanced towards the card before doing a double take. His olive skin paled and he quickly licked his lips as he calculated the best way to get out of the mess he'd got himself into.

'I'm sorry, sir, I didn't realise. It's just... You're going to the wrong lift.' The man swallowed and pointed to another lift set across the lobby. It had a single width silver door and surround, and was easily missed if you weren't specifically looking for it.

'Thank you. I haven't stayed here before and my assistant arranged the room.' The security-guy's own brows raised at that. 'She failed to pass on exactly where I was to go.'

'Of course, sir. Please let me know if there's anything you need. Anything at all.'

Cormac looked the man up and down, before nodding and turning to head to where he needed to go.

He glanced down at the card as he pressed the button, his head snapping up as the door slid open immediately. The operator inside jumped, scrambling to shove his phone deep in his pocket as he simultaneously tried to stand to attention. Cormac rolled his eyes before trying to step inside when the operator held out his hand to stop him.

'I'm sorry, sir. Platinum level only.'

Again, Cormac held up the card in his hand and the other man quickly nodded and stepped to one side to allow the Blake brothers access. Cormac glanced over to where the buttons usually were, surprised to see that there wasn't a list of floors as per usual. Instead, there were just two buttons, great big *platinum*—not silver—buttons side by side.

'Your card please, sir,' the operator asked, holding out his hand. Cormac hesitated before handing it to him and watched with James, both curious as to what he needed it for, as he slid it into the slot under the two buttons. A ring of light highlighted one labelled as *up*.

'Next stop, Penthouse,' the operator said as he pressed the lit-up button.

ALSO BY E.V. DARCY

The Royals of Avalone - Inheritance: Victoria
Buying Him: Victoria Part 1
Taking Him: Victoria Part 2
Keeping Him: Victoria Part 3

The Royals of Avalone - Inheritance: Henrietta
Beating the System: Henrietta Part 1

COMING SOON
The Royals of Avalone - Inheritance: Henrietta
Cheating the System: Henrietta Part 2
Defeating the System: Henrietta Part 3

The Royals of Avalone - Inheritance: Alexandra
Becoming a Queen: Alexandra Part 1
Playing a Queen: Alexandra Part 2

ABOUT THE AUTHOR

E. V. Darcy is a former high school teacher with a Bachelor of Arts in Imaginative Writing from Liverpool John Moores University.

She lives in the north of England with her husband and rather large–and very *spoilt*–dog, Jabba, who she rescued in 2015.

When Evie isn't writing you can find her binge watching her favourite T.V. shows, playing computer games, or walking her much loved dog.

Visit E. V. Darcy's website for more information on her latest releases and other titbits. Join her newsletter for sneak peeks, first to know about forthcoming releases and discounts on pre-orders!

www.evdarcy.com
Other ways to contact E. V. Darcy: